DEAD WEST

BOND OF BLOOD

J Patrick Allen

DEAD WEST: BOND OF BLOOD
An 18thWall Productions book published by
arrangement with J Patrick Allen
verba mea in minibus
desiderium meum
Cover by Jason Behnke
Design by Elisgraphics
Text Copyright
Bond of Blood, *Dead West*, and all related characters and concepts © J Patrick Allen
Series Edited by Nicole Petit

PUBLISHER'S NOTE

AUTHOR'S NOTE
All characters appearing in this work are fictitious. Any resemblance to real persons, living or dead, is purely coincidental. Except for Bill Hickok. He was definitely real—though not in the way he'd like us to believe. The author asks that you try none of the stunts you've read at home. Do not engage in shoot-outs, do not rob trains, do not contract with demons. Lastly, a tree of hanged-men will not ensure immortality. At the very least, it will make the neighbors complain until the cops show up. The author takes no responsibility for what happens next.

For Jennifer,
Madly and Deeply

Table of Contents

Amelia,

You want to know about the grave in Kansas? The cemetery it lives in is bordered on the East by a gentle river and on the West by an endless ocean of yellow summer grass that came up to my waist. This ocean, I remember, was dotted by tiny islands of trees. We did not open that grave, in the nowhere town between river and ocean. But it was opened for us and we stared into it, two men, a woman, and two children of age.

I was the one on the right, fourteen and certain I knew Right from Wrong.

If you were to look into the face of each person in our party I expect you would find the desires of each body written plain. On one man you would see a want of justice, and on another the need to serve. On the woman you would find open lust at what she spied within the grave. Within the girl beside me burned a vicious need for blood.

I stood apart from the rest. I think the only thing you would have seen on my face was a desire for conscience.

You're asking what's in the grave—and I'll tell you in time. But it needs a proper introduction, as does the man the grave belonged to. The open grave on that Kansas plain is not the beginning of this story. If I had to pick a beginning I would lay it at the night a creature visited my father and I in the little immigrant town of Hermann, Missouri. But you've heard my account of that story so I will spare you.

In fact, the only proper beginning I can think of is in Charlotte.

Chapter One

The House in Charlotte

There is a house in Charlotte, North Carolina which few have
seen the inside of. It stands cheek to jowl beside others like it,
squat and made of red brick with white details. The people of
the neighborhood understand it to be a club for gentlemen—a
very exclusive club. There is no brass plaque to announce its
purpose, no trail of high-class clientele waiting to enter. But
perhaps you've been on the porch, seen the small compass
rose scratched into one of the window casings. North, south,
east, and a crude skull where you would find west.

It was in this house that Samuel and I wintered. I said
goodbye to Hermann in August and we made a few stops for
business on the way. Once in Alton, Illinois and once in
Rossville, Tennessee.

I'm not sure what I expected of the clubhouse. Samuel told
me a little about the men that congregated there. At last in
November, with cold winds blowing in from the Atlantic, we
arrived in Charlotte. I huddled behind Samuel, pulling my
coat tight about me, while he rapped on the knocker. The man
who answered the door was the first of many unusual things I
would see in that house.

The man's skin was a reddish brown. He was long of chin,
long of nose, with a long sharp black beard. I wondered if
perhaps the man was Indian. He did not dress as I had been
told they dressed—rather than being stripped to the waist and
dressed in deer hide breeches he wore a suit of fine black
wool. The suit, like his face, was somber. The only effect of
color on him at all was a red silk sash which served as his belt.
The most unusual part of his garb was the strange headdress

he wore, a single scrap of scarf wrapped about his head to completely cover his hair.

"Suresh." Samuel nodded by way of greeting and Suresh stepped aside to let us in.

I stared agape at Suresh as I walked into the house, earning a cuff on the shoulder from Samuel. Suresh gave a knowing smile at the gesture and bowed to me. "We received your letter, Mr. Clayton. This must be Charlie Kirchner."

"Virgil home?" Samuel asked.

"Virgil is always home."

The house was dark. What little sunlight the overcast winter afternoon offered was blocked by sheer curtains and dampened by green wallpapers and wine dark wood paneling. Suresh guided us the short walk to the house's parlor. Bookshelves lined the walls, weighed down with hundreds of leatherbound volumes or with jars and bottles containing odd colored liquids and macabre trophies.

The fireplace provided the only real light in this room, and that was obscured by two wing-backed chairs set before it. A stuffed animal's head hung above the fireplace, though I could not make sense of what I was looking at. It appeared to be an eagle's head, covered in flush glossy black feathers, but it was easily twice the size of a man's head with a copper colored beak the length of a man's forearm.

"That Samuel's voice I heard?" a man called from one of the chairs, in an unfamiliar accent. A figure rose out of the chair, though it seemed a struggle. Like Suresh he was dressed in fine wools, though he had a bear of a black and grey beard which split to reveal a gnarly grin.

The man hobbled around the chair, leaning hard on a lacquered black cane. Out of the corner of my eye I saw Suresh twitch, almost going to him to help. The man was large, but in the way of men who were once barrels of muscle.

For all that, though, he held an air of dignity to him that was hard to miss.

"Let me get a look at ye, you stoic son of a bitch. If you've had any new injuries you'd never tell me."

"Better a son of a bitch than a Scotch bastard."

The large man gave him a playful shove and Samuel chuckled, hiding a smile. It was as close to a grin as I usually saw him give outside of hunting. The man took Samuel by the jaw and inspected him. "Letting the beard grow out?"

"Thought I'd imitate my boss."

"Bullshit. You're visiting the barber tomorrow aren't ye?"

"First thing."

The bear of a man had a bear of a laugh, slapping Samuel on the shoulder. After a moment of shared joy he looked over Samuel's shoulder and spied me, hiding away from them.

"Oh, aye, this must be Charlie. Now let me get a look at *you*."

He hobbled across the carpet, swatting Samuel away when the man tried to help him.

"By the mortal, of all the men in our little band to take on apprentice…" the man mused, fixing me with a long stare. He began probing me—pulled up my lips to look at my teeth, pulled down my eyelids to get a good look in my eyes. The inspecting hand bore an iron ring on it, identical to Samuel's, emblazoned with the compass rose and skull. He ran it along my cheek, cold and sharp, and I realized suddenly what he was doing.

He wanted to be sure that I was human.

"No tricks, Virge," Samuel said behind him. "I just wanted to take on an apprentice."

The old man, Virgil I supposed, snorted. "Orson I could see taking an apprentice. Daniel, certainly. Even Bonehill in his own way. But you…?" He turned to give Samuel a

10

piercing gaze.

"Boy saved my life."

"From what?"

"A witch's ghost," I said, finding my voice. "She'd stabbed him before she died and kept the wound from healing."

"That a fact…?" Virgil eyed me again. "How'd you do it?"

Samuel cut in. "Dragged me half dying into a Catholic church. Sussed out the priest would know what to do. Pulled her to the floor with bone ash while the priest got his shit together."

Virgil busted out his bear laugh again and slapped me on the shoulder, making my knees buckle. "All that then? On your own?"

"On his own, Virge," Samuel said.

I shuffled my feet on the woolen rug, not quite meeting Virgil's gaze. "Samuel saved my life first."

Virgil lifted a brow, a questioning look directed at Samuel. "That is what we're in the business of, more or less. Was it a creature?"

"Remember the river lore I asked about?" Samuel asked.

Virgil inclined his head.

"Charlie is the son of the man who hired me. Turns out it was a Nix. Boy's ancestors established a contract with the beast. First born son each generation for wealth and power."

The older gentleman tsked. "Bad business, trucking with that sort. If the father hired you, and the boy is here…"

I looked away, a lump hardening in my throat.

"I see," Virgil said gently. He cleared his throat and patted me on the shoulder. "Well boy, I guess we'll decide what to do with you when the others arrive. In the meantime, welcome to the Fraternal Order of the Knights of Charlotte."

Chapter Two

Daniel

There was an extravagance to the dilapidation of the house in Charlotte. The décor was fine, if old. The paintings were masterful, but faded. Some parts of the house, like the sitting room, were well-worn and cleaned. Some parts, such as the rooms upstairs, smelled stale with abandonment. Suresh showed us to our rooms. I stood by and watched as he saw to pulling sheets off the furniture in mine, as he slowly and methodically replaced the bedding and poured oil into the room's one lantern.

The bed was sweet down, the likes of which I'd never had before. When I crawled under the sheets that night I spent only a little while in fear of the new surroundings. Moonlight cast unfamiliar shadows on the wall, its strange alchemy turning trees to grasping claws and making the paintings grimace. A snort raised the hairs on the back of my neck, followed by the clopping of a horse's hooves on cobble. After that, the soft hug of feathers dragged me down into the kind of sleep that leaves the impression of dreams but no memory.

Days passed with busywork. I helped Samuel cast bullets—lead and silver for all of our various rifles and pistols. In exchange he took me out of town to the woods and taught me to shoot. We practiced on empty cans and dusty old whiskey bottles. He taught me to shoot birds, then rabbits.

In the evening I was allowed to read from the brothers' magnificent library. Histories. Folklore. Philosophy. Some of my favorites, I admit, were the dime novels: Cheap paper containing cheap stories of grisly murder and monsters most foul. Virgil would watch me as I read and laugh when my eyes went wide.

"These are just stories though, right?" I would ask.

He would smile and say, "There is a grain of truth even in these. Once or twice a brother has been saved by knowledge gleaned from this literary garbage."

Our second week there I awoke to laughter. Light trills of joy on the other side of my window. I crawled out of bed, mindful of the cold floor, and looked out. It was snowing— not a decent Missouri snow which sticks to everything and makes the whole world look like cake. It was a fitful Southern snow, which brings down only a few flakes that vanish in a breath. But children ducked horse traffic, running through the streets with their arms stretched out to catch the flakes.

I watched them for a long time. Most were younger than me, but a few my own age stood apart laughing and joking on their own. A coldness crept into my chest. I shook my head and turned away. As I did, I saw Samuel standing at the door watching me.

We stared at one another, blank, before he cleared his throat.

"You're up, I see."

I nodded.

"I have a few errands to run, and it's snowing out there. I thought maybe you'd..." He gestured helplessly with his hands. "C'mon, wash your face and throw some clothes on."

I gave myself a few splashes from the basin and ran a finger and tooth powder through my mouth. On a hook by the door hung my only hat and my only jacket. The coat was for a man, not a boy, and the hat was a ragged old straw hat that had survived the first trip out of Hermann, and the entire episode with the Nix. Suffice to say, it looked worse for wear.

I walked downstairs to find Virgil and Samuel in the sitting room, in chairs flanking the fireplace. They ate from a table laid out between the chairs. Suresh stood to one side, pouring coffee into a delicate cup.

"Charlie my boy," Virgil called. "Come have some breakfast. Suresh has prepared some wonderful sausage and grits. Have a cup of some of the foul tar he calls coffee."

"Never met a man who was this bad at brewing coffee," Samuel said.

"I have never met a man who complained this much while eating," Suresh said. His face was impassive, but I thought I saw just the barest flicker of a smile at the corner of one lip.

Samuel and I had a brief breakfast with Virgil and Suresh. I said nothing, my ears straining at the sound of children playing outside. Meanwhile, Samuel and Virgil discussed business.

"Any word on the others?"

"I anticipate Orson and Daniel will be here any day now," Virgil said, spearing a flat sausage patty with a tarnished old silver fork. "Bonehill sent a telegram a few weeks back from Houston. He will be with us in time for the meeting."

Samuel's head raised slightly at that. "Tom's joining us this year?"

"Mm, this will be the first year everyone is together in two…three years? I suspect he'll have some valuable information for our Bibles."

At that, I glanced at the mantle where Virgil and Samuel's copies of the book they jokingly called the Charlotte Bible lay. They were a study in difference. Virgil's book was hardbound and clean cut, with only a few loose pages of notes popping from between the pages and a brass lock holding it tight. Samuel's was loose leather binding together an unruly array of rough-cut pages, some of them actually bound in.

But the contents were the same. Each of the brothers were expected to keep a journal of their findings. Monsters

14

encountered, how to track them, and how to kill them. Rumors heard, folklore found, potions and powders to counteract the preternatural. I would often hear them say that the Charlotte Bible held salvation for a hunter.

We finished breakfast and Suresh took the dishes back to the kitchen while Samuel and I helped push the table back against one wall. Afterward, we said our goodbyes and moved out into the cold. I pulled my jacket close and shivered, staring at the children as we walked past. They in turn slowed to watch us.

"Reckon this is the first time they've ever seen a boy come out of that house," Samuel said after a few moments. He looked me over, taking a nip from his flask for warmth. "That all the coat you got?"

I nodded, folding my hands into it as I hugged it close.

"We'll have to fix that." He checked his wallet, blanching at what he found there. Then he began fishing through his pockets. "Should be enough to get you a jacket at least."

As we made our way through the streets of Charlotte something in a window caught my eye. I stopped to stare, pressing my hands against the glass, my breath fogging against it. Samuel stopped a few steps later and circled round to join me.

It was a bookshop, small and tidy, with an array of lovely leatherbound books of poetry and tomes of science and geography on the display. My mouth salivated at the thought of the feel of good paper and a sturdy leather cover in my hand. I had not had a book to call my own since long before we'd left Hermann. They sung to me.

Samuel hesitated. "I'm sorry, boy. We can't do it. They want too much money for those old things, and you need a new coat. Other things besides."

Slowly, painfully, he peeled me from the glass and we

continued on our way. To Samuel's relief a tailor in town happened to have a good wool coat, black and threaded through with blue, that had belonged to his son once upon a time. It more or less fit, only needing to be taken in around the chest. He promised to have it ready for us the next morning.

After, Samuel took me to a gunsmith. There he retrieved a package in brown paper and tucked it under his arm. We walked back to the Chapterhouse. Children still played in the hardly-accumulating snow when we arrived, and again they slowed in their play to watch us as we went past. I stopped, too, and watched them.

"Go on and play, Charlie." Samuel gave me a slight shove, but I resisted.

I shook my head.

"Nothing wrong with it," he said.

Again I shook my head. My throat tightened. Before he could speak I spun and ran for the door to the Chapterhouse. I flung the door open, throwing myself in, and immediately bounced off a man standing just on the other side. The man stumbled forward a few steps while I careened to the floor.

"Heavens!" The man said. "What's all this, then?"

I looked up. The fellow was portly, with a bristly red mustache that did not match his thinning nut-brown hair. He extended a hand and I saw it bore an iron ring like Samuel's, stamped with the compass-and-skull.

I stared at the hand only for a moment. Behind me, Samuel grabbed me under my armpits and hauled me to my feet.

"Apologies, Daniel. Usually the boy is more sensible than that."

I looked behind me to find Samuel frowning, his eyes creasing at the corners in irritation.

"Boy? You have a boy?" The man Daniel leaned in to inspect me. "He doesn't have your features. I presume he

16

takes after the mother?"

"I—I'm not his son." As first words to a man who would become a lifelong friend go, these were not the best. Hastily, I bent to pick up my straw hat trying to hide my blushing.

"Daniel, this is Charlie Kirchner. He saved me from a witch's ghost out in Missouri."

"A witch's ghost, is that right?" He began to curl the edge of his mustache with a knuckle. It seemed like an unconscious gesture.

I shook my head. "Samuel helped me kill a Nix. They're water fairies."

Daniel laughed. "I'm familiar. What information he has on them was likely gleaned from me?"

Samuel laid a hand on my shoulder and I looked up at him. "Thanks for the information. You were on the money with those iron slugs."

"I thought you said the person having difficulty with a Nix was an older man."

I swallowed. "He—he was. The Nix caught my father last year. It chased me clear to Minnesota before I found Samuel."

Virgil broke in, his voice barking from down the hall in the sitting room. "Close the damn door! You'll let all the warm out."

And that is how I came to be acquainted with Mr. Daniel Garner, the Charlotte Brotherhood's resident scholar.

Chapter Three

The Charlotte Conference

Daniel and I hit it off immediately. Perhaps because of the sheer amount of time I spent in the sitting room pouring over books, taking notes, and staring at woodblock illustrations. He shared a belief I had expressed to Samuel several times: monsters follow the laws of their own natures much as common beasts do, and these laws can be understood and cataloged.

I told him about the Nix and about our encounter with Ginny Catskill's ghost. In exchange he told me about trolls and phantoms, bog hags and bezoars, potions to protect against possession and how certain metals affect certain creatures. I could have stayed up all night every night listening to him, but I was usually chased to bed at the strike of nine.

Over the next few weeks more men began to trickle in. There was Franklin C. Jefferson, a tall man in expensive clothes whom Suresh later confided in me owned the Chapterhouse and whose inheritance financed our cause. Franklin had a habit of calling everyone "Sir," though with his thick Georgian accent it sounded more like "Suh."

Then there was Orson Foster-Dennings who arrived the day before my birthday. He had a boyish face and could not have been much more than seven or eight years older than me. Short and scrawny, the clothing he wore was shabby and worn but his gear was impeccable. You didn't need to know Orson long to realize he was a terminal optimist. Despite being an accomplished hunter, he walked about with a childish smile plastered on his round face and he seemed to think ill of no one.

On the occasion of my birthday Samuel surprised me with the brown paper package he had picked up from the gunsmith. I tore into it eagerly and found wrapped within a dark, polished Dance & Brothers revolver. I looked up at Samuel.

"This was yours," I said, wonder creeping into my voice.

He nodded. "I had the smith convert it for brass cartridges. Easier to load now. Also had the trigger loosened for you. Easier to fire, too."

"Samuel..."

"It's not much, but it'll get you started."

Virgil tapped his cane against the floor, watching us from the doorway to the sitting room. "A fine gift, child. Shall we walk to the woods and test it out?"

Samuel shook his head. "One more gift, first."

He pulled another package from the inside pocket of his coat. This was a slimmer package, wider. I took it carefully and peeled away the paper. Inside was a slim book with an ornately printed cover—a dime novel. *On a Springfield Evening: The Duel that Made Wild Bill.*

Again I looked up at him, eyes widening.

"I'm sorry," he said, shifting a little. He wouldn't meet my eyes. "It's not a big fancy science book, but it's what I could afford."

I clutched it close. A book of my own. A book that belonged to no one but me.

"It's wonderful, Samuel. Thank you."

That evening when I'd finished scrubbing the gunpowder from my hands I sat down and read the book. When the men chased me out of the room at nine o'clock I sat up and read it again three more times. Wild Bill Hickok, the man with a lightning arm. I imagined that he would have made a mighty monster hunter as well. I imagined myself a hundred times in

19

his place. Standing in the street, walking ten paces and turning. There, Davis Tutt would stand across from me and draw.

"Suh," I'd say in my best impression of Franklin, "You have impugned my honor!" I'd draw too, and we would both fire. His shot would go wide but mine…Mine would strike home.

I often stomped around the Chapterhouse reenacting that duel. Mostly, Samuel would roll his eyes and Virgil would chuckle. Daniel was happy to see me reading, and would regard me with a twinkle in his eyes. Suresh would simply mutter about never giving the enemy a chance to fire at you.

I began paying particular note to how I dressed. I made sure my shirt was always clean, and I frequently stopped to polish my shoes. Wild Bill was a famous dandy, and if I wanted to be like him it would not do to walk around looking like a vagrant. Franklin showed me how to comb my unruly long hair and on Christmas he gave me one of his beautiful long black bowties.

"A man must always look his best to make the proper impression," he would say.

Daniel presented me with a small blank book and a set of pencils. "Always observe, always record. What you see, what you learn, will save your life. It has saved mine many times."

So those next two weeks passed in a blur of conversation and imagined duels. The conference of Charlotte brothers was due to convene on New Years Day. On December thirty-first there was a knock on the door.

Tom Bonehill had arrived.

I did not see Bonehill's arrival. He rode into town at night, chased by a cold winter rain that would have made camping miserable. But the next morning he was there. When I came downstairs I did not find the men in the sitting room as I expected, but in the little used dining room. They sat around a long table while Suresh solemnly laid out breakfast.

Virgil sat at the head of the table and was the first to notice me as I stood beneath the arch leading into the room. He uncorked a bottle and poured a measure into his already-steaming teacup. "Ah, Charlie. Good morning. Come, have a seat."

There were a few good mornings from the other men, but the new arrival stared at me. What I saw sitting at the table in a sleep rumbled shirt, only one of his braces hanging on his shoulder, could have been Wild Bill come to dine with us. He had a narrow, angular face like Samuel's but the hair was sandy and fine and he wore a Van Dyke beard accentuating the knife sharpness of his features. The man's knife and fork held frozen above his plate while his cold blue eyes studied me.

"Who's the kid?" he asked.

Samuel cleared his throat of food. "Tom Bonehill, this is Charlie. Charlie, this is Tom."

Bonehill's jaw worked as though he got a joke no one was telling. "We taking in orphans or did someone sire a bastard in the war?"

Everyone but Samuel fell still. Samuel continued to dip his fry bread into egg yolk. It was up to me, then.

"I'm…" I cleared my throat. God, but it would be years before I ever felt like that voice exuded confidence. "I'm an assistant to Samuel. I help him, and he teaches me."

"What, that's the God's honest truth?" Bonehill looked at the others. Daniel wouldn't meet his eyes and Franklin seemed almost apologetic. "Surely that can't be right. Virge? You said we wasn't taking on any more than six. That was all the rings you found in that grave."

Virgil set down his teacup and folded his hands on the

21

table. When he spoke the burr of his accent came rougher than I'd heard it. "Tom, you know as well as the rest of us the dangers involved in our line of work. Charlie is quick-witted and clever, and should anything happen to Samuel he will make an apt replacement. There are only six brothers, but it does not hurt to have a contingency plan."

Bonehill seemed to think it over. Finally he gave a deadly soft chuckle. "Sam, you're the last person I expected to take on a brat. Garner maybe, Orson for sure. But you? Hell, the only person less likely than me would be you."

Samuel continued to eat without looking up. "Things change." The words were as cold and hard as the knife in his hand. He said nothing else.

Bonehill hesitated. Finally when he realized he wasn't going to get a rise out of Samuel he tossed his napkin on the table. "Things change, then."

The men resumed eating and Bonehill pointedly ignored me.

At noon the men convened to the sitting room and I followed them. Suresh arranged iron filings on the windowsills and drew the plush curtains shut. Then he pulled the double doors to the room shut, locking us in with the shadows, only the hearth to provide light. Orson and Samuel struck matches and lit some small lamps, further chasing the shadows to the flickering darkness at the corners of the room.

Virgil stiffly lowered himself into his chair by the fire and took a crystal decanter from the table beside it. "Suresh, if you would be so kind."

Orson took crystal glasses from one of the shelves and handed one to each of the brothers. When they came up one short for myself he vanished through the door to the kitchen and came back with a water glass. Suresh poured three fingers of brandy into each cup, including my own, and returned the decanter to the table beside Virgil's chair.

Virgil raised his cup. "With these drinks we close the circle."

"With these drinks we close the circle," the men intoned.

"May they bind us together as brothers," Virgil continued.

"May we stand together as one."

"The first sip honors homeland lost, our pilgrimage from the places of our youth."

"We drink to lost lives." The men took a sip, and at a glance from Samuel I did so as well. This was my first sip of scotch. It tasted like a forest carpet of wet pine needles in spring and the soft sweet glow of honey. The burn set me to coughing, but I kept my mouth closed and not a drop was spilled. It burned all the way down my gullet and my stomach wanted to rebel, but a moment later a pleasant warmth suffused my chest.

"The second sip honors the men who were lost when we were found."

"We drink to lost lives." Again they drank, and again I joined them.

"The third sip honors the sacrifices that must be made to keep humanity safe."

"We drink to lost lives." This swallow came hard. The words were too ominous to my ears, as I remembered Samuel telling me over and over again, *I'm no hero.*

Virgil took a deep breath and let it out slowly. "Who would like to begin the remembrance?"

The room fell quiet, only the ticking clock to fill the air. Orson shuffled and all eyes turned to him.

He raised his glass and said, "I watched a mother eaten inside out giving birth to a monster of a child. I was able to save the midwife and the doctor, but not her. She didn't deserve it."

23

The others raised their glasses. There were murmurs of "They never do," and "Amen." Everyone took a drink.

The dam was broken now, and the other brothers spoke up. Franklin toasted to the memory of the ghosts of soldiers lost in the war, whom he had had to lay to rest just three months gone. Daniel toasted to the memory of a librarian in New York he'd watched die screaming after opening a cursed tome. Samuel toasted to the memory of my father.

"To Florian Kirchner," he said. His voice was raw with self-recrimination "If only I'd been there."

"Amen, sir," Franklin said.

I sniffled, caught off guard by the tribute.

"To our brothers in arms," Bonehill said after a moment's silence. "To the boys who died to that horned beast the day we met Virgil."

"To the boys," the other men said in unison. It had the feel of a familiar, well-worn anxiety.

Again the room fell silent. I sniffled again and spoke up. "To Ginny Catskill."

The others turned to look at me, their faces half shadowed by the light.

"To Ginny Catskill," I repeated. "Who lost her way when the world did not turn out to be what she thought it was."

The men said nothing until Samuel took a sip from his glass. "Amen," he whispered.

"Amen," everyone but Bonehill said.

The meeting that followed was largely an exercise of small-scale bureaucracy. Minutes were taken, reports were given. The subject of these reports fascinated me—shambling nightmares in Houston, hissing abominations in the Dakota territory, slithering dreads in Cheyenne—but they were delivered with the dryness befit a banker's meeting. Still, I took notes. The results of research were given, the solutions to

24

many a fanged foe. I would later find my notes were far more extensive than even Samuel's, and it has been many a tense moment in the years to come where my curiosity on this subject and in these meetings would save our lives.

"There is one last subject of concern," Virgil said, shuffling through papers of notes he had made for himself. "It is an issue of finance. Franklin?"

"Esteemed gentlemen, if I may be frank."

"Please do," Virgil added, earning only an embarrassed smile from Franklin.

"Believing fully in our cause, you know that I have poured the entirety of my father's estate into our mission. This includes my inheritance and the sale of our many properties and businesses. Times being what they were six years ago I was not able to acquire even what I could in today's market. Still, it has been enough to see us through these six seasons since we began. Now, though, the water in the boiler is about to run dry. The coal is about to cool."

"Get on with it." Bonehill crossed his arms over his chest.

"I wouldn't use the word 'destitute,'" Franklin said. "But we must find a means of continuing. It has been a boon that we have managed to attain funding occasionally on the job, and each of you has done an admirable job of contributing to his own keep and care. That said, the time arrives fast when we will scarce be able to afford even the loans on this building, much less your individual stipends."

Orson leaned in, eyes wide. "What do you suggest? Would it help if we were each to sell what properties we still possess?"

"That would help stave off poverty for a time, sir," Franklin admitted.

"Like hell," Samuel growled.

I remembered the white house in Elizabethtown. It had

seemed all but abandoned, guarded only by the ghost of a slave named Solomon. Samuel didn't talk about the house, and in fact it seemed that he and the folk in the town were happily obliged to avoid each other. So it was that the fire in his voice took me by surprise.

Franklin cleared his throat, not meeting Samuel's stern gaze. "I am also working on some old family contacts. I believe I will be able to procure some shares in the Northern Pacific. Father was good friends with the company's head, a Mister Jay Cooke." He looked around, expectantly. When no one congratulated him on knowing such an esteemed individual he continued on.

The conversation quickly became noise to my ears, as the men discussed finances and methods of procuring funding. I wanted to go back to talking about the kinds of armament that could kill a Bollywag (what ever *that* was). To my relief, the clock struck three and broke the men from their spell.

"Gentlemen, I think we will convene for the day," Virgil said, forcing himself up out of his chair. "Suresh will have prepared a lovely supper. Go stretch your legs, and we'll meet for grub in an hour."

Someone opened the curtains and the doors, letting blessed light and fresh air in. I hadn't realized how stuffy the room had become until that very moment. Virgil limped from the room and Franklin followed, but Orson caught the attention of the remaining three.

"Boys," he said, his hands fidgeting with his suspenders. "You heard the news?"

"What news?" Samuel asked, stopping beside him at the arched doorway.

"It's about Barker Raleigh."

Samuel and Bonehill tensed at the shoulders, and I saw a flash of concern cross Daniel's worried face.

"He's…" Orson looked between the three of them. "I'm surprised you hadn't read it yet. He was shot dead by a U.S. Marshal maybe a week past. His men scattered, but his body was confirmed."

Samuel seethed quietly while Bonehill pounded a fist on the wall. Daniel looked down and seemed to pray for a moment.

I recognized the name of course. The papers had been screaming about him for a year and a half now. The Raleigh Gang was yet another in crowd of Confederate dissidents raising hell out west through brazen daylight bank robberies and train-jackings. Some were decrying him as an ulcer in the stomach of an ailing nation. Still others offered their support, spoke volumes of his bravery in standing up to a corrupt government. They wanted to fix him in the American consciousness as a kind of Robin Hood, and to that end their efforts appeared to be working.

One of the biggest points of speculation surrounding the Raleigh gang was what they did with their earnings. Certain newspaper editors had been working hard to let the American public know how some gangs distributed their money to the poor (despite apparent evidence to the contrary) and there were always rumors floating around in those days of bacchanalians thrown by some gangs after a successful robbery. But neither had ever been heard from the Raleigh gang.

Perhaps with his death Barker Raleigh was less Robin Hood distributing his ill-gotten wealth among the serfs, and more Captain Laffitte with a great treasure just waiting to be discovered.

"Did you know him?" I asked.

Daniel nodded. "When he was a young man, he served with us for a year in the war. The three of us were in a unit

27

together."

"Stupid kid," Samuel muttered.

"I need a drink," Bonehill said.

Samuel nodded. "Me too."

"I'll gladly drink to his memory," Daniel said. "But let's not forget he died by his own actions."

Bonehill nodded somberly, but Samuel looked away. Something in his expression bothered me, but I knew not what I was looking at. Not yet.

Chapter Four

Drawn

Suresh laid a hand on my shoulder, startling me back to the here and now. I looked up, trying not to show the fright on my face. He looked down at me with the same grim regard he showed everyone.

"Spying is not a very polite habit."

My gaze drifted to my feet and I mumbled, "Sorry, sir."

"…It is sometimes a necessary one in our line of work, however." When I looked back to him he was staring out the window at the subject of my fascination.

Samuel, Daniel, and Bonehill stood on the back porch staring into the distance. Their conversation was muted, quiet beyond my hearing. It was not their words which caused me to watch, though. It was what they were doing.

Samuel leaned a shoulder against a support post, Bonehill leaning on the opposite one by his elbow. Daniel stood between them, a hand stuffed in his pocket. The stances were outwardly relaxed, but there was a tension between the three of them, the tension of a cocked hammer. And each one, to the man, held their free hand out, dangling something, either by leather cord or delicate chain:

An iron ring.

"The rings the brothers wear often draw them to where they are most needed," Suresh told me. "They do not always work—most often the men must find danger on their own—but when the rings draw it is always important."

The rings did not hang as pendulums. Each tugged slightly in the same direction, seeming almost to be trying to stand. It looked much like I imagined dowsing must.

"They all point west," he said.

I nodded.

Suresh pulled some envelopes from within his jacket and passed them to me. They were still cold—they must have just arrived.

"Mister Garner and Mister Clayton have received correspondence from contacts looking to employ them. See that they get these."

I thanked him and walked through the kitchen to the back door. I could hear their voices now, though faintly.

"... could solve the money problem," Bonehill said.

Samuel sniffed. "As if we're entitled to the treasure."

"I'm afraid he's right," Daniel broke in. "It is not ours."

"The rings disagree," Bonehill said. "They're drawing us west—to Kansas."

There was a silence that passed between them then that I could only imagine was an uncomfortable one. Daniel, ever the voice of reason, spoke again.

"They are at least drawing us west. We could take the train together. More likely we are all being drawn to different tasks, but from this to the east of things it only *appears* we are all headed the same way."

"True," Samuel said, drawing the word out as if tasting what Daniel was saying. "We go west, see what we'll see. If we end up with a treasure..."

I opened the door. The sound of it was like the breaking of a hypnotist's spell. Each pulled from their reverie and turned to look at me. I bowed my head apologetically and held up the envelopes.

"Mail arrived."

"Good goddamn timing," Bonehill muttered.

Samuel ripped open his envelope while Daniel fussily pulled the flap up to ensure there was no tear. Each read their letters and exchanged looks.

"I'm needed in Kansas City," Samuel said.

Daniel nodded, "And I'm being called to Springfield, Missouri."

Bonehill spat a wad of tobacco juice into the grass. "Looks like we're headed west, then."

Chapter Five

Abilene

Arrangements were made, funding paid out, and train tickets purchased. A quarterhorse pony was purchased for me in Charlotte, along with some spare clothes for the journey. I adored the pony, naming him Dasher, and was constantly picking up clumps of grass or weeds from the roadside as I walked him away from the stable.

Franklin remarked that my hat was in a state of shambles and gave me an old slouch hat of his. "This will keep the sun out of your eyes, sir," he advised me as he adjusted my bow tie.

He, Orson, and Virgil saw us off, shaking hands with the others and patting me on the shoulder. In the months I'd spent in the chapterhouse it seemed I had come to be viewed as a kind of mascot or good luck charm. Better than a pet, I suppose, and I know now they meant kindly.

We rode away in mid-January, and I felt a thrill race up my spine. My own horse, a fine hat and fine clothes, and the solid weight of a six-gun strapped to my thigh. I could hardly have been in higher spirits. Beside me, Samuel rode quietly, chewing on the end of a rolled cigarette. Behind me I could hear Daniel humming. Ahead of me was Bonehill.

He was the striking image of a deadly gunman. His time on the border had affected his way of dress—he now wore a flat black hat with a wide brim, said to do well at keeping you cool in the merciless heat of the southwest territories. His jacket was double breasted, fringed buckskin, bearing the signs of patching and a few questionable stains. Though he bore a slick holster with a well-kept Smith & Wesson

American, it was the case strapped to the back of his horse that caught my eye. Long, flat, and solid. He rode with a hand rested on it, as though keeping it secure. As I would come to see on our journey he did not like to be kept away from it.

At the train station we led our horses in among mingling crowds of travelers. Two men in sharp suits made way for us so that we could check our horses with the stock cars, and then we were off.

I sat on my bench on the train reading my little dime novel for the thousandth time when I felt eyes on me. I looked up and around. Across the aisle was a family. The father, muddy-haired and tired, gripped two young boys (one ruddy and dark haired like his father, the other pale and red) who squirmed, on the verge of smacking each other over some puerile argument. A little girl sat across from him, though, and it was her eyes I felt.

She did not share her father's coloring. The girl was spattered with a coach gun's seeding of freckles all across her face and watched me with sharp grey eyes hidden from behind unruly red curls. She wore boy's trousers and a boy's shirt. I realized it wasn't me she was studying, it was my gun.

"That yours?" she said with a hint of awe.

"It was a gift." I nodded to Samuel who slept on the bench beside me, leaning against the rattling window.

My eyes began to sting a little at the sight of the father playing with the two boys. I looked away so the girl wouldn't see any tears.

"My da gave *me* a gun too." She jabbed her chest with her thumb. "Can you shoot it?"

Her accent immediately placed her as Irish. Her way of speaking was musical, almost dancing. The way her cadence rose and fell was hypnotic, and though she was filthy and dressed like a boy I found myself straining to listen to her, to

33

be able to hear even just a few more words.

I nodded again, blushing. I tried to speak, but found I couldn't and suddenly felt a fool. Certainly if my tongue were not caught I might have bragged that when Samuel placed six bottles on a fence I could hit five of them in short order. Naturally, this wasn't *always* true, but she wouldn't have to know that.

The girl extended her hand. "My name's October McMillen but everyone 'cept Da calls me Toby. Where're you headed? What's your name?"

Finally my voice returned. "Springfield. Charlie."

"Springfield Charlie?" Her lip curled in one corner. "Where's that?"

I cleared my throat. "My name is Springfield. We're headed to Charlie."

"I see," she said with no certainty that she did.

Business kept us traveling westward. We were detained in Springfield more than a month on a wild chase over flat countryside and along Missouri's threading brown rivers. Business was concluded at the open end of the tool in Tom Bonehill's mysterious case: a rare Whitworth rifle. Thirty-three inches long with an unusual octagonal barrel and even more unusual octagonal bullets.

We sighted the beast we tracked at the end of a long, rainy day and Bonehill dropped from his horse, prepped the rifle, and fired. The creature had to be 200 yards away—long odds for any rifle I knew of—and obscured by light underbrush, but the bullet found it and dropped it anyway. For days afterward I stared at Bonehill in quiet reverence, earning awkward glances from him. With Springfield at last concluded we made our way via train to Kansas City. That is when things turned sour.

Samuel's business there was grisly. We met his contact's

widow. She explained the man had been killed not but a day after sending the letter. I saw Samuel's eyes turn flat at that news. The color always seemed to drain from them when faced with news of death. He would be blaming himself already.

We avenged Samuel's friend, but at great cost. Samuel was left limping for weeks afterward, and Bonehill and Daniel were consigned to bed rest for three months. Often I would catch them pulling their rings off and threading them through with a cord or a chain. And always the response from the ring was the same.

West.

It was the end of May by the time we finally mounted our horses and headed west. Locals were only more than happy to tell us that Barker Raleigh had been shot and buried in a small town some miles south and west by the name of Rosewater. So it was, on a sweltering spring day, that we found ourselves standing over the grave of an infamous bank robber and guerrilla fighter.

The grave marker was wood and did not say much. *Barker Raleigh, died 1870*. At the bottom corner, someone had carved *BURN IN HELL RALEIGH*.

The men were quiet, each staring at the marker, each paying his respects. Somewhere far off a grasshopper sang and wind made the prairie grass sigh. I thought I heard a voice in that sigh.

"What?" I said.

"Any one of us could have had his fate," Bonehill said with, I thought, uncharacteristic introspection.

Garner shook his head. "We knew when a cause was lost." I heard the addendum he didn't say. *Or were smart enough to realize it was never worth fighting.* Garner struck me as being less of a Southern patriot than the other two. To my

35

knowledge he had never even owned slaves or farmland.

Samuel said nothing. He took a sip from his silver flask and passed it around to the others. Bonehill and Garner each took their turn and Garner handed it back to Samuel. With an almost religious reverence I rarely saw from him he tipped the flask and poured a libation on the earth above the dead Barker Raleigh.

"Check your rings," he said at last.

The three of them pulled their rings off and strung them. Judging by the sun I could see they dowsed north, northeast.

"Back the way we came?" I asked.

"More northerly," Samuel said. "Saddle up."

Our ride took us into Kansas and on to Abilene where we stopped for the night. As we neared town I saw a great dust cloud a few miles to the south and stood in my stirrups, pointing. An unfamiliar sound was carried to us on the wind—the thunder of hooves and the lows of the cattle. Cowboys shouted as they drove the herd on.

"What's that?"

All three men turned to look but Garner answered. "A cattle drive. Must be one of the first ones of the year, this early on."

He dipped a hand into his saddlebags and came out with a leather-clad brass spyglass and passed it to me. "Want a look? Here, be careful now."

I extended it and put my eye to the lens. After a moment's adjustment to the sudden leap in vision I began casting about until I could see the cattle. Hundreds of them, dark, with horns stretching longer than the length of both my arms. Men danced about them on ponies, guiding them.

"Jiminy!" I said. "Look at all those cows."

"Don't call 'em cows," Bonehill said. "Cows is just the

women."

I glanced over my shoulder at him, offering a smile of thanks. He spat in the dirt and ignored it so I planted my eye back on the spyglass. There among them I caught something that drew my attention. I guided Dasher to a stop and turned around to peer again. I saw it better this time, and I was certain of what I was looking at.

"There's a girl driving those beeves."

Bonehill snorted. "Women don't drive cattle, boy."

"Well, there's a woman driving this herd," I insisted.

Samuel guided his yellow horse around and came up beside me, holding out a hand for the spyglass. I passed it to him and he brought it up to his eye.

"I'll be damned, he's right."

Again Bonehill scoffed, rolling his eyes. "You don't have to lie for his sake, Sam."

"I ain't lying, Tom. There's a woman helping that drive." He seemed like he was about to say something else but shook his head, chewing over the words instead. Samuel collapsed the spyglass and passed it to Daniel.

"Let me see that," Bonehill said.

Daniel took a deep breath and reluctantly passed the spyglass to him. When Bonehill grasped it Garner gave him a disapproving look. "If you break this, I will break you."

"I didn't break it last time."

"You also didn't return it to me."

"I just wanted to see if I could..."

"I know what you wanted," Daniel said. "And I said no."

The two stared at each other over the device and finally Daniel let go. Bonehill pulled it open and peered through it. He chewed his lip as he studied the scene. The cattle were even louder now, their noise carrying clear in the hot dry air.

"Huh." Bonehill passed the spyglass back to Daniel and

turned about to Abilene again.

"He was right," Samuel said.

Bonehill shrugged.

"Say it." Samuel pulled his horse into motion and came up beside Bonehill. Daniel and I quickly urged ours on to follow.

Bonehill spat in the dirt again. "Fine, the boy was right."

I frowned at the two of them. Samuel's icy gaze was directed at Bonehill and Bonehill stared at the road ahead of us. I glanced at Daniel, jerking my head in their direction. Daniel shrugged as if to say, *God only knows.*

At mid-afternoon we arrived in Abilene, sitting low on the Kansas plains. The city was built in layers. The outermost layer was the stockyards, beginning to fill even now with beef product to be shipped east to Chicago, Boston, and dinner plates across the country. The yards gave Abilene half its distinctive smell, the earthy tang of cow dung.

The other half came from the second layer: The train yards. Until very recently Abilene had been the furthest point west on the map. The rail was slowly stretching further and further west, and new cowtowns were popping up on the map as convenient places for Texas ranchers to sell off their stock without driving into states like Missouri where cattle drives were outlawed.

The inside layer of Abilene was where the people lived and shopped. In those days the main road through town was bordered in false-fronted saloons, hotels, theaters, and stores selling anything a Kansas settler or Texan cowboy could need. Fine tooled saddle and tack, beautiful furniture shipped from the east, and, for the womenfolk, even finer clothes courtesy of the latest fashions in Paris. My eyes bulged at the sight of the fashionable women strutting about beneath parasols.

Behind the main drag was a larger selection of less sophisticated hotels, saloons, and theaters. Beyond even that were the small wooden homes that crowded together with no sense of order or border. Abilene in 1871 was a town of thousands, having reached the height of its popularity only the year before.

The men sent me to see that the horses were stabled and tended to by a livery that wasn't likely to rip us off. Meanwhile they took care of hotel accommodations and resupplying us for wherever the rings took us. The boys working the livery glanced askance at the rig on my hip but didn't say anything.

Samuel found me as I was leaving the livery, his arms loaded down with sacks of goods. "Take one of these, will you?"

I relieved him of a burlap sack and we walked companionably up the road to the hotel. Despite the location, the hotel was nice. It was quiet, the walls stomping out all noise but the distant clang of a train's bell. Everything inside was clean and the wood was polished 'til it shone. Stairs dominated the center, sweeping upward in a graceful arc to the second floor where most of the rooms were. Tables were arranged on the first floor where someone might get a quiet bite to eat or have a moment of rest before going back out into the bustle of the noisy town.

A gentleman, dusty from the road, stood at the counter haggling prices with the hotel's clerk. His accent was strange to my ears, refined.

"That man's accent..."

"English," Samuel said. "They like to buy up grazing land and send their boys out here to tend farm."

Samuel gave the man a cursory glance, then I saw his gaze turn. I followed the arc of his head and saw what he found more interesting than the man at the desk.

A woman sat alone in the little café adjacent to the clerk's desk, back straight, staring down at an arrangement of cards before her. Her clothing was practical, though likewise dusty from travel. Despite that, she sat like a queen delivering mercy and judgment, her sun-gold hair the only crown she needed.

I caught a glance of a card as she pulled it from the deck and laid it flush on the table. It was the flash of a color, hand drawn. A woman in white sat upon a throne in the card. Before Samuel knew what I was doing I crossed the space to her. She looked up as I crossed, eyes flicking from me to Samuel and back.

"I've not seen playing cards like that, before," I said coming near.

"They're an older sort of playing card," she said scooping up the cards laid across the table with a nimble hand. Her voice, like the gentleman's, was cultured and refined. Each syllable was silkily enunciated, and the sound of it made something in the back of my head stir pleasantly. I realized she must be a companion of the Englishman.

She began shuffling them again. Again her eyes flitted between me and Samuel, though he kept his distance. I observed her clothes—a plain white cotton blouse and skirts divided for riding—and had a sudden spark of realization.

"You were leading that herd of cattle!"

She laughed and when she did the sun glinted off a pin on her breast, a cross wrapped in roses and vines. "You saw that, did you? That I was, young man."

"I've never heard of a woman who did that! One of our traveling companions didn't believe me when I saw you. He said it ain't done."

She glanced at Samuel, and I saw his brows knitted in concentration.

"Not him. Another companion of ours."

The woman gave a wry smile and tossed a curl of yellow hair over her shoulder. "It isn't done by most, but then again *I'm* not most. M'father had no one else to send and I insisted t'was better I look after his investments than a stranger."

She resumed shuffling her cards and they made a messy sound in her hands, though she neatly interlaced them.

"What's the game you're playing?" I asked. "Solitaire?"

"Something far older than Solitaire, my friend." She glanced at me sidelong while she shuffled. "I'm telling my fortune."

"With cards?"

She nodded. "It is an excellent tool of self-enlightenment and discovery. Would you like to try?"

Chapter Six

Portents and Futures

I glanced back at Samuel. He shrugged, keeping his distance, though I saw something like a guarded interest in the way he half-turned his body toward us. I settled in the chair across from her and she extended her hand.

"Mrs. Madeline Irving."

I took the hand, thinking briefly of doing something stupidly chivalrous with it. Instead I shook it. "Charlie Kirchner."

"Lovely to meet you, Charlie. Cut these, would you?" She laid the shuffled deck before me and I lifted the top half and set it to the side. Mrs. Irving put the bottom half atop the top half and shuffled once more. Then she began taking a handful of cards and laid them in an arc in one smooth gesture.

"Feel the cards, Charlie. Yes, with your hand just above them. Good, now pick one. Now lay it face up on the table."

She gestured to the place before her and I laid it there. A young man with a bindle over his shoulder stared up at me from the card. The top and the bottom were labeled so that anyone looking at the card could read it.

The Fool.

"This card represents you," she said, matter-of-factly.

I felt a blush of protest rise in my cheeks, but she gave a full, red smile to cut at my embarrassment.

"It doesn't mean you're a simpleton, Charlie. The Fool is a good card. Especially placed as it is."

I did not see what difference placement could make, but I let her continue.

"I think you are at the beginning of a new journey, or

you've recently started one. Does that sound familiar?"

I nodded. My mind played out the events of the last year—leaving home, chased in the night by a Grimm's fairy tale. Leaving home one last time, joining with a band of monster hunters. She studied me, waiting for me to say anything, but I could think of nothing worth saying.

Without prompting she took another card and laid it across the first. A man in a dark cloak stood, mourning three spilled cups before him, while a river barred him from a castle in the distance. The label marked it as a Five of cups. Mrs. Irving paused, fingering the card, her face thoughtful.

"What does it mean?" I asked.

She took a deep breath. "Nominally, there are tribulations that you have experienced or are about to experience. Either this trial is ahead of you, or perhaps it has passed and you have yet to deal with the consequences of your actions."

After a moment she gave a shy smile and gestured to the card. "But look, even though he's lost three of his cups, two stand behind him unnoticed. Never forget that you always have something to rely on."

I glanced at Samuel, smiling. I knew when everything else went wrong I had Samuel and he had me. He watched, but with a far away look as though he was not really present in the moment.

Mrs. Irving laid out more cards. "My, you've come a long way. I think your tribulations must have been in the past."

"What do you mean?"

"I think that you have experienced some loss in your life recently, but it looks like you're strong and you are working through it as best you can. This card here can also mean that you have new friends to lean on. Perhaps they're your two full cups."

Mrs. Irving smiled again and leaned in close, and I

43

followed suit. She whispered to me, "Would you like a try at your future?"

I nodded eagerly and she began to lay out cards again. She tapped the cleft of her chin with her index finger, thinking. "Well, I believe you may be a boon."

"How is that?"

"It looks like you will be of vital importance to a friend in coming days. Keep close to your companions, for they will need you."

She laid out more cards and frowned. "This, though…"

Dark robed men marching about brandishing keys or swords. People tortured, men hanged.

"I believe there is a dark figure in your future." She laid out one more card, an eleventh card, and placed it across the dark figure. "You have it in you to change your own fate, but you must be wary."

Mrs. Irving let out a rush of air, her whole body suddenly sagging under released pressure. "My, this was an involved reading. I saw one like it once back home, but I've never performed one myself."

"How long have you been doing this?" I asked.

"Only perhaps a year, and mostly for myself."

Ominous portents, dark futures, unusual readings. I felt a thrill up my spine.

"Samuel! This is fun. Come have your fortune read."

A laugh skittered out of Mrs. Irving's mouth as she exhaled a held breath. Samuel glanced at the two of us, hesitating. One hand rested on the edge of his suspenders, fingers dancing as he thought the offer over. He must have made up his mind, as a moment later he crossed to stand by the side of the table. She lifted her hand for him, gracefully, and Samuel swept his hat off in genuine chivalry and took her hand in a firm shake.

I saw a flicker of tension at that touch, at the corners of her mouth and in the set of her shoulders. The feel of the air between them shifted from warmth to cold. Again her gaze flitted between Samuel and me. She was on guard.

Samuel took my place at the table and I stood near to watch, but Mrs. Irving shooed me away. "Readings are private business. You could affect the outcome."

I stood well away. By now the man at the counter was finished haggling with the hotel clerk and he came to stand beside me. We watched in silence as she guided Samuel through the same steps she'd led me through. Her face was delighted warmth but the angle of her neck and the stiffness of her shoulders told me that wariness was still there.

Samuel's mood darkened as the reading progressed. I caught soft trails of sarcastic remarks. He rolled his eyes at something she said and he broke away early, standing. He collected his things and swept across the room past me.

"C'mon, Charlie. We can't waste any more of our time on this nonsense. We got work to do."

I watched him thunder up the stairs, his face a flashing black storm cloud, and I felt hurt swell in my chest. I looked to Mrs. Irving, but she did not meet my gaze. She sat at her table, staring numbly at her cards. At last I walked up the stairs to join Samuel.

We entered the hotel room to find the other two Knights sitting across from each other. Bonehill occupied a ladderback chair, his jacket open and his mouth closed in a tight, white line. Daniel sat at the edge of the bed, gnawing at the end of his thumbnail, his eyes fixed on the middle distance.

Samuel grunted when he saw the both of them, but I stopped to assess.

"What's wrong?" I asked.

45

Daniel unfolded a newspaper that had been laying in his lap and read the headline aloud.

"Raleigh Gang Robs Dubuque Iowa Bank in Boldest Raid Yet." He gave a deflating sigh and summarized the article. "Three dead, four wounded. None of them were gang members."

Samuel laid the sacks of provisions against the washstand. "So his boys are still a pack of whoresons. What of it?"

Daniel tapped a line with his finger. "Barker Raleigh, previously thought shot dead in Rosewater, Kansas, spied among the robbers."

Samuel snatched the paper from Daniel's offering hand and I stood on the tips of my toes to catch a glimpse of the broad sheet. The paper included an artist's interpretation of the events: a pack of men armed with smoke spewing guns and covered in masks.

"If they were all wearing masks like that," I began slowly, thinking the words aloud, "How would anyone know it was Raleigh?"

Bonehill fixed his eyes on me and I shrunk away, expecting to be scolded for asking a dumb question. Finally he shook his head. "Probably took his mask off for a moment."

"Someone's probably impersonating him," Samuel said.

"Our rings are still pointing north and east," Daniel replied.

Bonehill snorted. "In the direction of Iowa."

Samuel stroked his thumb along a scar traced through his beard at the jaw. He shook his head. "We've got supplies for the ride. We get rest tonight and leave in the morning."

Chapter Seven

The Pursuit of Rumor

Dime novels and other tales of adventure are ripe with stories of heroes crossing paths with the foe by chance, or tracking him over miles using nothing but broken twigs and muddy footprints to see the way. In truth our work is often more mundane than that. So much of the life of a Charlotte brother is the pursuit of rumor.

The rings went inert in Dubuque, a sign the brothers often take as little more than falling onto the right path. We canvassed the Iowa border town for rumor, starting at the bank that was robbed and poking about taverns, hotels, and dance halls for leads. Some claimed it was Raleigh, others said it was an imposter. Some said he was masked, others said his face was revealed for God and all His angels to see. He was whole and hale, or full of holes. One carpenter tried to tell us he put his finger through the hole where Raleigh had been shot in Rosewater.

Most of what we gleaned from our collected investigations was less than useless. I took notes with a little book bound in loose scrap leather, a gift from Daniel, and afterward he and I would pour over the things reported back to us and try to trace the common threads between stories. More than being detective work, the exercise taught me how to think. It was the beginnings of honing my eye for detail into a straight edge that would serve me in adulthood, slicing through nonsense and idiocy to bare the truth beneath.

Our stay in the little town lasted only a day. One thing nearly everyone agreed upon was that the Raleigh gang traveled west into Nebraska. It was not a trail of broken twigs and muddy footprints that we followed—it was a trail of pilfered train cars, of stages meant to carry payroll to distant army posts, of banks with dynamite-blasted doors. And at each of these steps we learned it was a trail of blood.

Raleigh's gang was not quick or neat in their bloodshed. They were particular about who they killed, choosing only the sternest of Union supporters. But in each instance there was a brutality that I have only seen matched by the most inhuman creatures. Bodies riddled with lead long after death, corpses dragged for miles behind horses, men tortured with knife and hot metal until they gave up safe combinations.

Of the latter, death seemed a mercy. I was sure they gave up their secrets long before the torture ended.

The trail carried west for half the state before curving south, and then east again. A week and a half in Nebraska, after two days riding easterly, the men decided to try plowing ahead of the gang's wake and try to catch them rather than catch up. We rode hard east in the direction the trail pointed through Burwell, Pawnee, and Lincoln until we came to the bustling city of Brownville rubbing cheeks with the Missouri river.

News carried fast, and one of the first things we learned upon entering town was that a stage had been hit the day before, perhaps twenty miles out of town. People were nervous. Armed and discrete, the brothers split to search for any sign of the gang. We had a handful of descriptions and names now, each meticulously noted in both my journal and in a similar journal carried by Daniel.

Samuel and I worked together and, not for the first time since leaving Charlotte, I felt conspicuous with the heavy weight of the smokewagon strapped to my thigh. We checked saloons, Samuel picking up a small drink or a beer at each stop to blend in. He would stare in the mirror behind the long bar, studying the afternoon drunks while I stole surreptitious glances at the men at their tables.

After three bars we found nothing of note and moved on to a pair of livery stables occupying the same street as the last saloon. Samuel asked the hands questions, trying to pry for answers. "Saw a group of men come riding in. There a county fair? No? That's odd. Maybe I'll ask them myself. You ain't stabling their horses, are you?" And so on. Each time I studied the men, looking for any signs of duplicity or nervousness. As near as I could discern, they told the truth.

Samuel sent me to poke around a bank along the main drag, look around for anyone on the list. I returned to find him waiting in a cafe with lunch. We slowly ate sandwiches and a plate of beans, and Samuel drank cup after cup of harsh black coffee, trying to brace himself against the earlier blast of alcohol. And all the while we watched.

After an hour of watching we saw the business at the bank begin to pick up. Men began to enter through the front door every few minutes. I counted.

"Ten men and one woman have entered. Three men have left," I said after a half hour.

Samuel ran his thumb along the scar on his jaw. He took another sip, mulling over what I'd said. "Noticed that. Weren't a line in there when you checked in?"

"No, sir."

"Business shouldn't be taking that long." He left the coins for our meal on the table and got up. I followed him out and across the street. I could feel my pulse quicken with each step closer and foolishly my hand kept straying to the butt of my pistol. Even when I caught myself, I kept my jacket open and pulled away from the holster the way I'd seen Samuel and Bonehill do just before a fight. Images from *On a Springfield Evening* played over and over in my head and I began to feel a surge of fear and excitement rush through my veins.

Once out of the sun, though, the bank was disappointingly mundane. Men (and one woman) waited their turn while one harried teller tried to calm down a portly man in a fine sack coat and red vest.

"No, sir! It will not stand. I demand see the bank's owner."

Listening to him talk reminded me of Franklin.

Under pretense of waiting in line we kept an eye on the scene, and I soaked in every detail. The teller seemed to be the only body holding the bank down, and he sweated under the fierce scrutiny of the man at the counter—a Mr. Boddard judging by the anxious stumblings of the teller. The men seemed sweaty, and more than one carried the dust of travel. Other than the argument at the counter the only other noise was the faint buzzing of flies and the tick of the clock standing in the corner.

While we waited two more men came in behind us and I glanced at them. The tension in my blood had lowered, bringing me down off of a high of fear and alertness. The simple normalcy of the scene eased me back to earth.

Mr. Boddard seemed to realize he was not going to get what he wanted—a sizable withdrawal of all his savings in the bank—until the return of the bank owner, and stepped out vowing to come back and bring hell with him.

When he was gone one of the men muttered, "Thank Jesus for the end of *that*."

The woman, whom I realized now was wringing her hands, stepped up to the counter.

"I'm so sorry," she began.

"Sorry for what?" the teller asked.

Another man stepped through the door. "Terribly sorry that we'll have to relieve you of your money."

Samuel swallowed. "Mother of—"

As he spoke, other men in the bank began to pull on masks. The man immediately behind the woman gently pushed her to one side, revealing his own pistol trained on the teller.

"No one likes heroes," the new arrival said. "No one likes—shit."

He came toward us, laughing. I looked up at Samuel unsure, and I saw dread realization drawing on his face.

"Lieutenant Samuel Henry Clayton. That *is* you!"

When Samuel didn't respond the man remembered his manners and lowered his mask, laughing. "It's me, Barker! Holy God, but it's good to see you."

Chapter Eight

Blood and Rain

The atmosphere warmed by degrees. The men did not holster their weapons, but they no longer regarded us with hostility. Raleigh clapped Samuel on the shoulder with his free hand and draped that arm around Samuel's shoulder.

"Lieutenant, I'm mighty pleased to see you." He pinned Samuel close and gestured with his gun to some of the men. They continued to threaten the teller while their boss addressed Samuel.

"How are you holding up, old boy?"

Samuel's eyes were wide and the corners of his mouth drawn down. "How the hell are you alive, Barker?"

Raleigh laughed. "*That* is the question, ain't it? You 're looking a little ragged around the edges." He fingered the collar of Samuel's jacket. "Need work?"

"We paid respects at your grave," Samuel said.

Raleigh leaned in to Samuel, his voice practically purring. "I pay well, old boy. You know the, eh, industry I'm involved in."

"I'm familiar," Samuel said, his voice stiff.

"You're a crack shot."

"You'd know better than anyone." Samuel's eyes wandered down to the man's chest, but Raleigh laughed.

"I suppose I would." He gripped at the spot on his chest where Samuel had glanced. "Water under the bridge, old boy! Come on. There's lots of gold to be had."

Samuel stared at the other man for longer than I liked. Meanwhile the other men were herding the teller into the back room. One of his boys, a tall man with a broad shoulder shoved the teller in and slammed the door shut with a right arm that bulged disproportionately large compared to his left. The building shook when he pulled that door shut.

"I ain't interested in gold."

Raleigh gave Samuel a critical eye, taking in his shabby, road worn clothing and his disheveled grooming. "No, I suppose you're not. But I can offer something better."

"Murder?"

"Vengeance." The word sounded delectable on Raleigh's tongue. It sounded like he was tasting a succulent soup after a long day. "I have an end game. It's gonna be big."

Samuel's gaze was diamantine. He stared the other man over with that hard, piercing look that I'd seen whenever he studied a potentially dangerous or potentially useful thing. My heart stopped. I believed Samuel was leaning toward useful.

Samuel opened his mouth. Something cracked across the street and a man standing in the doorway crumpled against the counter.

"Gunfire!" someone shouted.

"The thunder's here!" Raleigh shouted. He went to one side of the door and peeked out.

A firm hand gripped me and I gasped. It was only Samuel—he shoved me to one side behind a table and out of the way. Men began firing and the glass at the windows shattered. Holes appeared in the wood walls, casting shafts of smoky light. The man with the one large arm punched through one window, heedless of the shards cutting his glove.

As I watched, Samuel drew the blue and brass Remington at his side and pulled the hammer back. One shot nailed a masked man at the counter. The next tore into a bandit storming out from the back office. The third struck the big-armed man nearby in the shoulder. By then they realized Samuel was shooting at them.

Samuel grabbed me by the scruff of my collar and dragged us both out a shattered window. We fell out onto the street, a swarm of bullets humming over our heads. I found cover behind a barrel, trying to rein in my pounding heart and ragged breath.

This was not how I'd pictured grand gunfights.

There was no slow building tension, no men falling under the first hail, and no crowd to cheer us. No, instead what I had was the stink of blood and acrid gunsmoke. I had the taut-wire fear. I had the taste of bile threatening to run up my throat.

My shaking hands pulled the flap of my holster aside and I found my revolver by touch. I pulled it out and tried to pull back the hammer, but damnit my hands wouldn't move!

A bullet clipped the barrel and a hole exploded beside me, showering me in rainwater and splinters. I screamed.

Someone was calling us out. Someone was calling *Samuel* out.

Raleigh yelled, hidden beside the window we'd just come through. "These men are your brothers, Lieutenant! Each and every one fights the war we fought. Remember that, Samuel, old boy?"

I clutched at my chest, my breath racing out of control. A moment later a hand gripped me and pulled me away from the fight. It was Daniel, yanking me down an alley and behind the bank. I followed after him, the Dance revolver feeling like dead weight in my hand.

The crack and bark of gunfire continued from the front of the bank unabated, but behind us I began to hear a pounding. Daniel dragged us around another corner just in time for the door at the back of the bank to burst open, scattering across the dirt alley and crashing against the wall of the building across.

Raleigh's men poured from the door, some casting about

with guns, canvas bags slung over their shoulder. Others offered a shoulder for shot men. Raleigh followed among them and they retreated, scattering to the four winds among the buildings of the alley. The last vanguard followed out, covering the retreat. He dragged the teller with him.

As Daniel and I watched the man shoved the teller against the wall and pulled the trigger on his pistol. The gun fired once and the wall was painted in red and bits of skull. I gasped, the sight too horrible. The robber's head jerked up, peering in our direction.

"Come out or you're dead." He paced toward us.

Daniel shoved me to one side and came out, his hands up. The robber raised his gun even as I watched.

The alley filled once again with the bark of gunfire.

The robber looked down at his own chest, blinking. A spot blossomed and grew on his chest, red as his mask. The smoking revolver shook in my hands and I realized where I was—standing between the robber and Daniel, faster than I had realized, faster than the robber.

He collapsed to the mud, so much meat. I dropped to my knees and evacuated my stomach of the sandwich and beans.

"Charlie," Daniel said. "Charlie, we need to go."

He collected me, and my discarded revolver, and pulled me from the sight of that carnage. I barely felt the beginnings of warm summer rain spattering my cheeks. Two drops, then four, then six, and soon a gully washer.

We found Bonehill in an alley behind the restaurant where Samuel and I had eaten earlier. He was climbing off the roof, the Whitworth's case slung over his back. Rain hammered the leather case, but didn't seem to infiltrate it. Samuel joined us a moment later, swinging around a far corner, shoulders tensed and his face anvil hard. When he saw me he relaxed a little.

"That was a good shot," Daniel said to Bonehill.

"I don't think it was a killing shot." Bonehill hopped off a barrel and landed with both feet on the ground. "Saw him hobbling out the back on the shoulder of a friend."

A man wandered down the wrong alley a moment later, coming into view. Before my hand could even reach the butt of my pistol I heard the scrape of leather and the click of three hammers. The stranger and I both were surprised to find three swift guns trained on him.

A dark patch of wet formed at his crotch and he hobbled off, mumbling apologies. Daniel was the only one to flush with embarrassment. Each holstered his piece in a way that was characteristic to themselves: Samuel's was the no-nonsense stab of the gun back into his holster. Daniel would slide the barrel of his Colt along the length of the leather to get a sense of where the gun went in. Bonehill twirled his at the trigger guard and it landed snugly home.

I gawked at that one. "Wow! Can you teach me to do that?"

Bonehill blinked. "What, this?" He pulled it out again, twirling. His arms moved fast, up, down, around, and the gun spun and twirled. Bonehill tossed it in the air and caught it, still spinning. One final flourish brought it home again.

He grinned at my face and nudged Samuel. "If you're not careful I may steal that one away from you."

Samuel said nothing, too lost in his own thoughts.

The four of us stood in a circle, under an overhang against the rain. I hugged my jacket close and we watched each other.

"Shouldn't we go after them?" I asked.

"We're not in a hurry yet," Daniel said. "The wet ground will make it easy to track them and we need to get our heads on straight. Sam, what did you see in there?"

"Barker."

A sweat visibly broke out on Daniel's brow and Bonehill

spat in the dirt.

"Thought I heard him hollering, but thought I must'a been wrong," Bonehill said.

Samuel shook his head. "It was him alright. Apparently alive and well."

Daniel stepped forward. "What did you hear? What's his plans?"

Samuel held up his hands in a placating gesture. "He didn't exactly open up his heart. Said he was after vengeance."

I tilted my head at that. The others looked thoughtful over the news, but I still felt lost. "Vengeance? Did something happen to him during the war?"

"The war is what happened to him," Daniel said. "Most folk were left devastated by the war. Battle took a piece of them and burned it. Others, though...Men like Barker, they thrived. He was in his element when charging his horse into Yankee formations."

"If he wants vengeance, it's *for* the war, not because of it," Samuel said.

Bonehill nodded. "Clayton's right. If anything he'll want to restart the war out here."

Daniel pulled his hat from his head and began flicking the rain off of it. "The wounds are still raw out here because of men like him and those abolitionists."

Bonehill pulled a flask similar to Samuel's from his jacket pocket and took a swig. He passed it around. Each man took a sip, staring into distant memory as they did. Each was reliving his private war. The flask came to me, and I had no war to relive, but I took a sip to their health, and because I wasn't often offered the flask. It burned peat and pine needles and I almost spit it out, but when I forced myself to swallow, my whole chest flushed with a pleasant heat.

The strike of a match beside me was Samuel starting into a

57

cigarillo. He watched the others for a moment while he puffed it up to a decent glow and then took it from his teeth. "Let's hit the trail. Daylight's burning."

Chapter Nine

Crossroads

The rain continued until sunset and finally abated in time for the last rosy rays to appear over the horizon. We followed the stamp of a dozen sets of hoof prints for several miles west of town, and then going south. The ride was quiet, the men were singularly focused on the task of tracking Raleigh and his gang before a posse could catch up to us—one was already being called at the town sheriff's office when we left Brownville.

The trail became confused when we hit that sunset, though.

We reached a crossroads around the time the sky cleared and Samuel called a halt, his voice sharp and commanding. I wondered if this was the voice he'd used as a cavalryman. The sight we found surprised me. The remains of a fire lay smoldering and wet in the center of a crossroads. A lone tree decorated one corner of the cross and from it hung a man, his face swollen and purple, his tongue lolling out.

It was the man I'd shot back in Brownville, hours ago.

I stared, dumbstruck, at the body. I remembered the frightening buck of my pistol, of the sight of his body falling, of the rain peppering him as he lay in the mud. Now, black flies swarmed him where he dangled.

I was so caught up I did not hear Daniel approach. "It's him, isn't it?"

I nodded. Suddenly brought back to myself, I turned away and consciously closed my agape mouth.

"Tsk. An unusual degree of decomposition, as if he had been there for days. Go get your notebook, Charlie. Observe the site and note down anything you see. Giving your mind something to do helps you process horror." Daniel gave me a kindly pat on the shoulder and moved off to where Bonehill was inspecting something.

Bonehill leaned into Daniel and I heard him mutter, "The boy freezing up on us?"

Ignoring the body, ignoring Bonehill's jibes, I took out my notebook and started to mark observations. Now that I was paying attention to the whole scene something felt off that I couldn't quite put my finger on.

Wind howled over the lonely Nebraska plains, and somewhere distant I could hear a coyote calling evening reverie. *Time to wake up, boys.*

I paced the site. Tracks coming from the east and split going north, west, and south. Some were old, stamped in while the dirt was dry. Many were fresh, coming in and milling about. I found where the horses were brought off the road and tethered by the tree—the grass was trampled here, and there were more than a few road apples mixed into it.

So the Raleigh gang rode in under cover of rainfall, tethered up their horses for a rest, and what? Did the fire come first or the hanging? In either case, the man was hung on the opposite side of the tree from the horses. I guessed not to disturb them. I gave the body another cursory glance and then determined not to look at it again. Instead I walked to where Samuel was squatting by the remains of the fire, in the center of the crossroads.

I knelt opposite of him, tapping my pencil against my teeth. Something struck me. "It looks old."

Samuel grunted.

"But we can't be any more than an hour behind them," I added.

"You're close," he said. "Not asking the right question, I think."

I tapped the pencil against my teeth again, considering what the right question would be. "Why would you build a fire *in* the crossroads and not away from it, where you're less likely to get trampled? Why would you build it in the rain?"

Samuel tapped the side of his nose and gave a grim smile.

Another important question sprang to mind. "Why are we chasing him, Samuel? He's not a monster."

Samuel barked a laugh. "Oh, he's a monster alright. Never met a man as eager to spill Yankee blood."

Daniel and Bonehill joined us by the ashes and Daniel said, "We're chasing him because the rings led us to him."

Bonehill shook his head. "Clearly we were brought here to secure Raleigh's horde for Brotherhood coffers."

I glanced between the two of them and back to Samuel. He stared at the ashes, hard. Something in the set of his jaw told me his thoughts on the issue differed entirely.

"But he's not..." I waved my hands impotently trying to find the right words. "He's not otherworldly. He's just a man, not a creature. He's not fairy, he's not devil, he's not spirit or anything of the sort. He's just a man."

Samuel finally spoke again. "Maybe we was meant to join him."

Nearby, Daniel blanched.

Samuel continued on, never taking his eyes off the ashes. "Takes a monster to hunt a monster, and he's hunting the biggest monster we ever fought."

I felt my frown deepening. Daniel was shaking his head and Bonehill visibly sunk into deep contemplation.

"Daniel," Samuel said, "You enlisted when Ohio infantrymen raped and killed your little sister. And you, Bonehill. That plantation had been in your family for generations when a Massachusetts platoon burned it to the ground. Your grandfather was awarded that land for services

61

rendered in the Goddamn Revolution."

Bonehill looked away and Daniel seemed cowed.

"You can't tell me the U.S. Government wasn't the biggest Goddamn monster we ever fought." Samuel pushed off the ground and walked to his horse, climbing in the saddle.

He turned the horse toward us and stared us down. "We got three sets of tracks going in three different directions. Judging by the number of them, they didn't just split up. All three roads seems to carry the whole damn host."

"So they doubled back," Bonehill said. "Repeated their tracks to throw us off."

I stared at the ashes, at the spot Samuel had seemed so fixated on while he'd sat before me.

Bonehill spoke up. "So they doubled back. Tripled back, I guess. They made three different trails to throw us off."

Samuel shook his head. "We'd have seen the tracks if they did."

I reached into the ashes, heedless of the mess.

"I watched Charlie shoot the man hanging in the tree," Daniel said. "We saw him fall."

"So what?" Bonehill asked.

Samuel seemed to know where this was going. "Look at the purpling on his face, Tom. The man was clearly living when they hung him."

I began to sift through the ashes, curious. There was still a heat there, but the fire felt hours dead, not the minutes it must have been.

"And they didn't tie him up," Daniel added. "I wonder what that means."

"It means they didn't tie him up," Samuel said with an edge to his voice. "The longer we sit around jawing the further away he gets!"

My hand fell on something cool, something metal. I

62

pinched it in my fingers and drew it out. It was a coin—an old one, unevenly molded and imperfectly circular. One side held a circle like the one I'd found in Minnesota, the circle Ginny Catskill had used to call up Retribution. The other side bore a crude impression of a devil, squat with wings and a spiked tail. The edge of the coin read *HE WHO SO CALLS ME CALLS ME WITHER.*

"Calls me whither where?"

The other three fell silent in their bickering. I looked up to find each man staring at the coin in my hand.

"Where the hell did you get that?" Bonehill asked.

"It was in the fire."

Faster than I could track, Samuel was off his hand and over to me. He smacked the coin from my palm and it sailed, landing in the drying mud. Coyote howls again pierced the dusk air.

I stared up at Samuel, disbelieving. He glared at the coin, but there was something else there. His nostrils flared, his pupils shrank. Betrayal?

"Samuel, I—"

He held up a hand, cutting me off.

I saw Bonehill's eyes bulge. He tipped his hat back to air off his scalp and gave a low whistle. "So that's why we're chasing him."

Daniel tottered over to where the coin fell, pulling a handkerchief from his pocket and gingerly picking it up off the ground. "How do you suppose our young Raleigh came into a calling coin?"

Relaxing, Bonehill thumped his forehead with the heel of his hand. "*That's* how he made the multiple tracks."

"He must have been using it to evade the law for months," Daniel said. He meandered back to his horse and pulled a wooden box from his saddlebags, dropping the coin in with a

63

hard clank. With the kind of disgust one would have catching a mouse, he clicked the box shut and locked it.

"Well, the world is starting to make sense again," Bonehill said.

While Daniel and Bonehill discussed the coin I watched Samuel walk to each of the three forks of the road. At each one he dipped his hand into a hoof print and brought it to his nose to sniff it. North, then west, then south.

"That's an idiotically frivolous use of such black powers," Daniel said.

"We both served with the man. Idiot is a good word for him."

"He's going south," Samuel announced, cutting them off.

Out of curiosity I followed after him and repeated the test. A hoof print from the southern fork smelled like mud. I jogged to the western fork and tried it. The smell caused my nose to wrinkle. Bad eggs.

"That's sulfur," Samuel said. "The northern and western trails must have been made by Raleigh's new business partner."

"South then," Daniel said.

"South," Bonehill agreed.

"South," I said.

So we turned south, following their hoofprints while the ground still held them soft. After hours riding they veered from the road and we followed them through the countryside by a more obscured trail of flattened grass and the scuff horseshoes left on stones. In the distance I spotted the lazy feather plume of an idling train's smokestack. My stomach lurched when Samuel pointed at it.

"They headed that'a way."

I wondered, riding toward the still form of the locomotive, if the grim faces on the men surrounding me meant they feared the same thing I did. But as we approached, all nightmares of another train robbery and another massacre disappeared.

The train itself was a simple ironhorse, a utility machine with only a single car latched to it, meant for hauling fuel. It was stopped in its inspections of the tracks, and the engineer seemed more than a little surprised when we rode up upon them.

"Seen any men riding this way?" Bonehill asked. "Several of them. Red bandannas?"

Samuel clambered off his horse, poking around the grass, a stone hush of concentration falling over him. Daniel kept close to me.

The engineer shook his head. He was a man of middling years, dark hair well on its way to gray, and his skin wrinkled and browned with a life of honest work. "Not a thing. When d'you think they came this way?"

"Perhaps two hours back," Daniel said. "Three?"

That startled me—had we really lost an hour or more?

The engineer doffed his cap, wiping at the grimy sweat glistening on his brow. He took a contemplative spit of chaw and said, "Afraid I hain't seen nothing. Only been here 'bout quarter an hour my own self. Stopped fer supper."

Bonehill and the engineer talked for a bit longer. It had the outward appearance of small talk, but I recognized the subtle hints—he was hunting for clues. While they talked Samuel continued to prowl about on foot, drawing nervous glances from the engineer, and Daniel began pulling books from his saddlebags. I knew he'd kept a few tomes for himself in those considerable bags, but the amount of them revealed, spine-up, when he lifted the flap of one leather bag startled me.

He sifted through books, checking them against the Charlotte Bible which lay open across his saddle. Sometime

65

when I hadn't been looking he had copied the crossroad coin into his book. I nudged Dasher closer and peered at the notes he was checking. The drawing was detailed, showing nicks and marks, and hatched to show relief and shadow. A fair hand with a pencil, and I'd never known.

"They're riding the rail." Samuel stood full upright, turning to us. "Burning daylight."

Bonehill tipped his hat to the engineer and I snagged the reins of Samuel's horse as we rode up to him. Samuel took the lead, jumping quickly back into the saddle and we were off again, following the railroad. We would follow it for several days to come.

We rode those rails clear to Abilene with no further sign of Raleigh and his boys. They were gone like pipe smoke in a gale.

Chapter Ten

Intentions

The early hours of the morning are a dangerous time to be caught alone with no company but your own thoughts. Dawn had not yet begun to smile on Abilene while I sat over my watch, my mind's eye revisiting the scene in Brownville over and over again. I studied my hands, searching for any trace of the powder that had ejected from the gun, for some sign of the sin I had committed with them.

Samuel also seemed restless, even by his own insomniac standards. He snored terribly, but often that snoring would slip into silence and I'd hear an unsteady breathing. Other times he would awake with a start and a choke of fear. It was during that pre-dawn black, when I felt at my lowest, that he woke up.

I heard him shift and looked to see him sit up at the side of the bed. He groaned, digging at his eyes with the heels of his large hands. When he was done he leaned his elbows against his knees and stared at the floor. The hotel still slept around us, though I thought I could hear the distant buzz of Daniel's snores.

"I'm taking over watch," he said, standing. Samuel washed his face at the basin and replaced me in the chair, exchanging my Sharps for his Henry.

He pushed me along by the shoulders without another word, nudging me toward the basin. I poured myself a cup of water and stared at it. I glanced at him to see him already sinking into a listless trance. With no further encouragement I downed the water in three gulps and crawled under the covers.

Sleep did not come easily. Every time I closed my eyes I could smell burnt powder. I saw a man sink to his knees in the mud, watched him lay his face down in the alley's sludge. I didn't realize I was crying until I sniffled.

"What?" Samuel asked, shook out of his torpor. "What is it?"

I couldn't roll over to look at him. I snuggled my face close into the dirty hotel pillow and mumbled, "I killed a man."

He shot to his feet. "What? When? Why didn't you wake me?"

"In Brownville, I mean."

"Christ almighty, don't scare me like that."

Silence fell between us again. He resumed his silent vigilance and I stared at the night-blackened ceiling, trying to find the words to assuage my bleeding conscience.

"I'm going to hell, aren't I?"

He stirred again, yanked once more out of his thoughts. Samuel's mouth worked, looking for a response. He crossed his arms and looked out the window. "Do I look like a preacher to you?"

"Thou shalt not kill," I said in persecution of my own life.

"It was just a bank robber."

"He was a human being."

"…Sometimes you have to do wrong to do right, Charlie."

I sniffled again. I wanted to tell him that was itself wrong. That the world should not be that way. "We're the good guys. Aren't we supposed to be better?"

"This world is no place for the better man. The sooner you learn that, the better."

I heard the strike of a match, smelled the sweet smoke of the cigarillo's leaves. He said nothing else for a long time, puffing at it. I opened my mouth to speak again and he cut me short.

68

"Get some sleep, Charlie. Only an hour or two 'til dawn.'"

I came down the stairs of the hotel early that morning. Bonehill and Daniel were eating breakfast in the little café to one side of the first floor. My gaze cast about, but I did not find the two things I was hoping to see: Samuel and Mrs. Irving. I supposed it was a vain hope that she would still be here after a few weeks' time.

Pulling up a chair to their table, I helped myself to some bacon and eggs from a plate in the center and the man working tables poured me some coffee.

"Where's Samuel?" I asked.

"Left before dawn," Bonehill said. He glanced at Daniel, who was a less than solid breakfast companion. For the hundredth time Daniel had books laid out on the table and ate over them as he read. I did not understand how the man could simultaneously read four books while making notes in a fifth.

I also did not understand how he did so while eating bacon and leaving not a single grease stain on their yellowed pages. He *did* reach for a pen, though, and started to nibble on it before he realized it was not bacon.

Bonehill ran a biscuit through the yolky remains of his eggs. "Finish your damn breakfast, Garner. *Then* research." He turned to me. "He left the damn light up all night reading those damn books."

Now that I thought about it, Bonehill's eyes did look a little sunken and bruised, but then so did everyone's. I was starting to take it as a hazard of the occupation.

"Wither. I know that name," Daniel muttered almost to himself. "I've heard it before, but I've checked everything I can think to check. There's nothing in Aethelstan's *Catalogue*, nothing in the Sigsand manuscript, nothing in *L'Blasphématoire Rituels*. If I were home I could perhaps

69

consult *The Celestial Compass*, *Ars Goetia,* or even *Ars Magia.*"

"We'll find something," I said, hoping I sounded helpful. The bacon was good, pleasantly crispy with an almost candy-like sweetness to it.

Daniel responded to my encouragement by releasing a long held breath. His mustache fluttered with the deep sigh and he sank into his chair. He absently dipped a biscuit in his coffee and chewed on it, dribbling coffee across his waistcoat.

"Slept in late," Bonehill said with a hint of reproach.

I glared at my plate, unable to look at him. "Hard time sleeping."

"We ain't in a business kindly of the lazy."

My cheeks burned. "I wasn't being lazy. I—"

"You what?"

"I can't sleep," I protested. "It's just…"

The door opened and a figure stood shadowed by the gold morning light, his thumbs tucked in his belt. He looked around the room slowly, head moving with a hard purpose. When his gaze rested on us he started toward our table. Each step was measured, confident, with the slight jangle of spurs.

No longer backlit, the shape of the man resolved into sight. Aged to the prime of his manhood, the fellow had long curly hair beneath a flat-brimmed hat and long drooping mustaches. If I didn't recognize him by the hair or the quality of his dress I might have immediately recognized him by the two colts slung across his waist in cross-draw holsters.

"Wild Bill," I said with what little breath was left to me.

There was an immediate shift behind me. Daniel sat upright again, brushing crumbs from his waistcoat and I sensed a taut-wire tension forming in Bonehill even without looking at him.

Hickok sensed it too. A hand drifted too casually to one

70

gun, fingers dancing over the butt. "My reputation precedes me. Good morning, gentlemen."

Daniel returned the greeting and Bonehill said nothing. I stared openly, absorbing every detail of him. The corner of his mouth tilted up at my expression.

"How can we help you, sir?" Daniel said. He rose, beginning to offer his chair but Hickok deferred.

"Gentlemen, as you may be aware, I am the sheriff of Abilene." He gave a none too subtle flash of the star beneath his jacket's lapel.

I think the two men behind me nodded. I gasped, "You are?" A sheriff of the busiest cow town in the country on top of everything else. Imagine!

He gave a bourbon warm laugh. "That I am, son. And as the sheriff it is my duty to learn a little bit about interesting new arrivals." His face resolved into something altogether harder. "And to inform them that Abilene is a firearm-free city."

That taut-wire sense came even stronger from Bonehill. There was a moment's quiet, cut only by the clearing of Daniel's throat.

"Certainly, sir. We would be happy to acquiesce. We were unaware of the law and had no intention to cause trouble. We suspect our stay will not be long, besides."

Daniel stood and began to unbelt his rig, giving me a sharp look until I remembered to do so myself. Hickok seemed offput by my handing him a full gunbelt and the heavy Dance revolver.

"This is some lightning for a boy your age."

My face flushed. "I know how to use it sir." It was hard not to trim the edge of regret from my voice.

He took the belt without a word, and accepted Daniel's and then the reluctant Bonehill's.

"I'm made to understand these are not the only guns you carry." He nudged his head towards the stairs, and turned to walk toward them simply expecting us to follow. "Though I find myself curious how it is you slipped into town without seeing the signs instructing all men to leave their guns with my deputies."

"We didn't come in through the main thoroughfare. We came in along rail," Daniel said.

"Yet no one at the station stopped you."

"We didn't come in by train," I added.

Hickok turned, halfway up the steps, to look down at us. His face was imperious, a judge demanding explanation.

Bonehill finally spoke. "We're bounty hunters. We been trailing prey."

Hickok's eyes took us all in, glancing at me only briefly. That look he gave me said it all. *Awful young to be a bounty hunter.*

"If you believe a wanted man to be in Abilene, your first duty will *always* be to come to me." He started back up the stairs, the click of his boots hammering home each syllable.

"That's not our thinking, Mr. Hickok," Daniel said. "We've been trying to follow them for days now, but the trail seemed to go cold. We're resupplying and reassessing our options."

We crossed the walkway overlooking the hotel room and Daniel slotted the dull colored key in the lock and opened the door. Across the room he opened the closet and allowed Hickok to take possession of his coach gun. Bonehill reluctantly gave his Whitworth over. Hickock's eyebrows rose in sharp surprise when he looked inside the case.

"Keeping this beauty fed in lead must cost you dearly."

"It's worth it." Bonehill's voice was as flat as his face. He already looked queer without his pistol, but the effect was doubled to dangerous effect with that face.

My hips, my soul, felt lighter without it. I didn't meet his eyes when he thanked us for our cooperation. Hickok explained our guns would be available with his office when we were ready to leave town and he excused himself.

We listened to his footsteps disappearing down the stairs and then perceived the ghost of the door's closing outside. Bonehill and Daniel stepped to action at once. The scholar found a large buck knife among his possessions and firmly belted it on and Bonehill pulled a cloth wrapped package from his bags and removed a Derringer, dropping it into a pocket on the inside of his jacket.

"Samuel's not going to like this," Daniel said, a finger playing over the knife.

Bonehill shook his head. "Damn cowboys have to ruin things for everyone."

"Charlie, go find Samuel, will you? Let him know to disarm."

I stepped lightly, and was soon downstairs and out the door. The town sounded so much busier than it had when we were through the first time. Even this deep in the city now I could hear the sounds of thousands of beeves in the stockyard, the clang of bells, the whistle of trains. Nearby foremen shouted orders to their men and women scolded hung-over husbands, children at play shouted and hollered. The noise gave Abilene a pulse, made it sound *alive*.

As I swung the corner around the door I drew short, nearly running into someone. "Well if it isn't Charlie Kirchner! Graham, this is Charlie Kirchner."

My eyes rose and widened. Madeline Irving stood before me, beautiful. She wore a dark violet dress trimmed in the latest style with a collar clear to her jaw and a bustle to accentuate her figure. Sunlight dappled her face, streaming

73

through the lace of her parasol. She regarded me with playful eyes.

"A pleasure to see you're back in town, Mr. Kirchner." She extended a hand to me, bearing a large signet ring of some kind, intended for a man. It bore the relief of a nine pointed star enclosed in a circle. Now, as an adult, I realize I was meant to shake it. I was not as astute as a child. Stunned and at a loss, something else set into place and I took the hand, bowing over the knuckles, and kissed it. Mrs. Irving whooped a surprised and delighted laugh.

"He's a proper gentleman, Graham."

"He is, Mrs. Irving," Graham intoned without emotion.

"Have you proven a boon to your friends?" She asked me. I was distracted by the way her long, gloved fingers nimbly spun the parasol. It caused shafts of morning light to dance before her and lace shadows to sway across her features.

I shook myself out of the trance and shrugged. "I'm not sure. Not yet."

"Well keep an eye out. Your friends may not realize how much they need you just yet." She paused, a small furrow forming on her brow. "Is your tall friend around? The dark one?"

"Samuel?"

"Samuel, yes that's it. Is he around?"

"I'm running to find him. We didn't know Abilene has laws against carrying within the city, so I have to tell him to go to Sheriff Hickok's office. Oh! I got to meet Wild Bill!"

She laughed, a sound like the chiming of bells. "Did you now, darling? I've only spied him a few times myself. He's a dashing figure in his long coat and with that lovely hat."

Unconsciously, I adjusted my necktie. If I became dressed as he did would women call me dashing?

Mrs. Irving leaned in close enough for me to smell the

violet soap she washed with. "Are his intentions honest?"

"His intentions? What do you mean by that?"

"Your friend is a dark man I saw in the cards. Something hangs over him. Discover whether he has honest intentions."

"He's..." I looked away from her. Samuel was not a bad person. The idea was impossible to me. Today I realize how naïve that thought seems but that is the way a child loves: with their whole heart, ignoring all sin. "Samuel saved my life."

She laid a gentle hand on my shoulder, pulling me from my thoughts. "Darling, are you staying at this hotel again?"

I nodded.

She pulled away, her voice becoming bright and musical again. "Then I shall surely see you around. Come along, Graham."

She walked inside, Graham trailing just behind her. I shook my head to clear the fog from it and dashed off to find Samuel.

Chapter Eleven

High Stakes

After a few hours searching I found Samuel at the post office. He was hard at work chasing rumors and I saw by his barren waist that Hickok or one of his deputies had already visited him. We rejoined and I tried to draw him into conversation but although he stood beside me he was leagues away.

Having my notebook with me, I started to help him in his hunt, jotting down things people said and the way they looked as they said it. All my life I've had a doctor's eye for detail—yes, even back then—and I knew you could learn a lot about a person by how they held themselves as they spoke, not just what they spoke. I had not yet learned there was a science to such deduction, but I was piecing it together by slow instinct.

There was not much of substance to learn. Yes, of course Barker Raleigh was dead. No, the gang had carried on without him. Should we even really be calling them the Barker Raleigh gang? And when we found people who believed he was alive the help we got was spurious at best. They shot and buried the wrong man. They shot the right man, but he was alive and dug his way out. Raleigh made a pact with the devil and charmed the Marshal into shooting his *deputy* and thinking it was Raleigh.

You think dubiously of my dismissing these thoughts. Frogmen roamed the waterways hunting little boys; witches could call down exotic spirits and make manifest nightmares. Chimeras hunted America's heartland for cattle and men, and yet I dismissed these ideas. Seeing some fantastic things come true does not mean all fantastic things are true, and besides I have always been suspicious of that tone of voice particular to the superstitious. Even when their superstitions have been proven true.

Even with rumor swiftly flying at the speed of rail, there was not much of use here that I could tell. Yet still I recorded everything in my notebook in case we could fit the pieces into a sharper picture later.

When we walked the city we returned to the hotel. As we neared I spied the shapes of Daniel and Bonehill leaving, stretching. Bonehill saw us first and stopped to await us. Daniel waved when he saw us approaching.

"We were going for a drink, and to collect our thoughts," Daniel explained as we drew near.

Samuel grunted and shook his head. "Not a bad idea. I could use to sit a spell."

We walked the block looking for an establishment with the particular qualities the men desired. Someplace clean but not falutin'. Someplace low class, but not wild. Someplace quiet, with cheap drinks of a modest quality, and maybe a little music. Samuel found the place first.

A false front gave the building the impression of a grand two-story establishment. Curling sapphire lettering scrolled across the second story of the front proclaiming *THE BLUE BEAVER* and *fine drink, dining, music—faro, poker, roulette.*

"Blow me down," Samuel muttered to himself.

I looked up at him. "Do you think it's the same?"

He snorted. "What are the odds two fool men would pick the same gaudy name."

Sure enough when we entered we found surly Zachariah House wiping an empty table clean. He was a grizzly of a man, bald with a fire red beard and broad shoulders. Each footstep he took was brick solid, knocking the floorboards loud. But he walked with a limp I had not noticed before. He glanced up at us from his work, doing a quick double take.

"Welcome gentlemen." His voice was a smoky rasp. He

77

peered at us a moment longer and tucked the rag into the waist strings of his apron. House looked more finely dressed than last I'd seen him, wearing a good pinstripe shirt with a separate collar and silky arm garters.

"Get you boys something to drink?"

Bonehill and Samuel claimed one of the unused tables. Daniel and I were only a moment slower, he opening his Charlotte Bible while I curiously eyed the rack of poker chips sitting on the table.

"Red-eye," Bonehill said, slouching into his chair.

"Beer," Samuel ordered.

Daniel tipped his hat to the bartender. "Do you have any Madeira?"

"The hell is Madeira?"

"I'll take a brandy, then."

I glanced at the others and back to House. "Whiskey?"

"He'll take a cup of water," Samuel corrected, giving me a sour eye.

"Got some lemonade," House offered.

I looked back to Samuel, trying to give him my most effective puppy-dog eyes.

"He'll take a lemonade, then."

We all settled at the table. Bonehill took the deck of cards as I was reaching them and began absently shuffling them.

"Whiskey," he muttered. "Honestly."

"I can drink it," I replied, trying not to sound so defensive. He snorted. "Sure."

"I can. Tell him, Samuel."

"Choked fire the last time I gave him a hit from my flask." Samuel tipped his chair back and brought his hat down over his eyes.

Bonehill was joined in laughter by a pair of well-dressed gentlemen at the next table over. We didn't have much of a wait given the few customers. Besides the proprietor and us there were perhaps six other men, and one of them appeared to be a piano player on break. He sat at the piano putting all his appreciation and concentration into the rolled cigarette in his fingers.

House arrived with our drinks soon after, laying everything down before us solid enough to slop some of Samuel's beer over the side.

"Say, boys, you look familiar. We met before?"

I opened my mouth but Samuel beat me to it. "Don't reckon so."

He gave us one more inspection, thinking it over, then began to nod slowly. "No, I suppose I'd know it if we'd met."

When he walked away the piano player began rattling off something jaunty on his ill-tuned piano. The extra noise gave us the proper cover and the three men leaned in to start talking.

"Find anything?" Bonehill asked Samuel.

"Rumors of rumors. One man swore he'd run off for New Mexico, another that he'd seen him walking the streets of Kansas City not two days back. Three men still swore he was dead but that thought's dying quick."

"Maybe Mrs. Irving can help us find him," I suggested.

Bonehill and Daniel looked at me questioningly.

"Fortune teller he met," Samuel explained.

"Legitimate?" Daniel adjusted his spectacles, seeming suddenly much more intent on the conversation than his Bible.

Samuel shook his head. "Bunkum. Some trick with playing cards." Though I was unsure even he believed the words he said.

"Tarot? Really?" Interest sparked in Daniel's voice. "I had not thought it had crossed the Atlantic yet."

"She's English," I said.

"I suppose that explains it. A friend of mine in London

speaks of the rising popularity of the subject at parties." Daniel pulled his specs from his nose and began to rub them clean with a handkerchief.

Daniel lapsed into silence, giving his attention to his Bible rather than his companions. Samuel seemed to nap, only rising occasionally to take a deep quaff of his beer. Bonehill sat in companionable silence to Samuel, methodically shuffling the cards. Thinking I should take a cue from Daniel, I began to pour over my notes from the last several days looking for any inkling, any hint of where the Raleigh gang might be.

I looked up, something occurring to me. "I think he'll stay around here," I announced. "In the Missouri, Kansas area that is."

Turning, I watched Samuel for any acknowledgment, any notice. He remained still, leaned back in his chair. After a moment he grunted, though it sounded more like he might be clearing his throat. He leaned forward long enough to take his mug and tilt back a long swallow of beer. Foam clung and popped in his mustache.

"Well?" I asked.

The wrong fish took my bait. Samuel remained quiet and Daniel answered, "It's a solid hypothesis. His gang has generally never strayed more than a few days ride north or south of Kansas or Missouri."

I stabbed a page of my notes with a finger. "And according to newspaper reports most of it's clustered around the state border. I think they have a hideout somewhere near the border."

"A hideout?" Bonehill crooked an eyebrow, watching me over a cup half-raised to his mouth. "This ain't a dime novel. Bandits don't usually have a single hideout. They go to ground wherever's convenient."

Samuel grunted again. Defeated in purpose and theory I fell silent.

As afternoon turned to evening the room slowly filled with cowboys and rail workers. Men stained with dung, dust, or grease filed in and took tables or spots at the bar. A saloon girl I recognized as one of House's old whores came in and started helping to serve drinks. Like House she was dressed in a considerably better state. Abilene had been good to them. And like House she did not recognize us. I felt mingling relief and disappointment.

Men looking to play cards gave us dirty looks for taking up a table but starting no game. When one came over to ask if he could grab the chips, Bonehill stared him in the eye and began to deal cards between Samuel, Daniel, and himself. The man walked away grousing.

"That gold has to be heavy to haul around everywhere, and, that we know of, they don't spend much of it," I said.

Putting away his Bible, Daniel took up his cards. "Where does one stash such a large amount of gold and valuables?"

"A hideout," I suggested again as I poked sullenly at my cup.

"You don't shit in your own well," Samuel said. "Bad idea to stow your goods so close to where you go to ground. Raleigh's smart—he'd hide it somewhere no one would expect to find him and the boys."

"But somewhere easy to reach from wherever he is," Daniel added. "The boy's theory isn't so far off."

"So they're local because they have to bury their gold," Bonehill said, rolling his eyes. He muttered something about pirates under his breath.

A voice rose, feminine-sweet and musical, drawing near. "Burying is impractical. Think of how often he'd have to dig the haul back up just to add to it."

81

I turned in my chair and the three men turned with me. Madeline Irving approached from a nearby table in a creamy orange evening gown that accentuated every curve and complimented the hue of her skin and hair. She gave us a wicked smile that matched the white of the strange beads around her neck and passed her closed parasol to Graham, who stood dutiful at her side, as always.

"Is there room for another player, loves? I'm told I'm quite good with cards. I promise to play honest—see? Nothing up my sleeves." She turned up her hands, encased in long pale gloves and opened the cuff of her sleeves for all present to see.

I glanced back at the others. Bonehill and Daniel were quickly covering up agape expressions. The legs of their chairs barked on the wood floor as they made room for her at the table. Beside them Samuel made no move. I recognized the clench in his jaw.

"How are you, Charlie? Mr. Clayton?" She settled as a cloud into her chair and spent a moment arranging her skirts for modesty. When all was well Graham assisted her in scooting her chair up to the table and she laid hands on the cards Bonehill dealt her.

He said nothing so I spoke to make up for the gap in conversation. "Good—both of us. We're both good. It's good to see you, Mrs. Irving. I was telling our traveling companions," I gestured to Daniel and Bonehill, drawing a severe look from the latter, "—all about your fortune telling skills."

Mrs. Irving laid a delicate hand on her breast, looking all about. "'Tis just a hobby, picked up to pass time in the dull parlors of London, I promise. I've been made to understand Americans bear a certain healthy skepticism toward the mystic."

"We're less skeptic than you'd think," Bonehill said

flipping a card from the stack onto the table.

Everyone took turns throwing in chips. The game was impenetrable to me, though I was apparently the only one.

"So you'd consider yourself open minded," she said, batting her eyes at Bonehill.

A cheesy grin split his knife-sharp mustache from his pointed beard. "I like to keep lots of things open—my mind, among them."

"Christ," Samuel muttered under his breath dropping his cards on the table. "Fold."

I wasn't sure if he groused because of his hand or because of Bonehill's shameless flirtation. The game continued in circles, chips exchanging hands quietly until Mrs. Irving suggested they play for pennies. The coins remained distributed even among them with the exception of Samuel. As the night wore on his pile dwindled and his mood darkened. By the fourth round of playing for money he was mercilessly grinding a good cigar between his teeth and all the while Bonehill and Daniel fell over themselves to pour drinks or trade banalities with Mrs. Irving.

"That's a curious brooch," Daniel said, leaning in to drop his wager in the pot.

"A souvenir of travel," Mrs. Irving said.

His brows rose. "You've been to some curious places. If I'm not mistaken, that is a Rosicrucian's pin, emblematic of membership. They are quite hard to come by, as their owners are loathe to surrender them."

"I'd heard it was such, but I was not sure it was authentic. What do you think?"

"I think it compliments your complexion, ma'am. You wouldn't be an alchemist playing an elaborate ruse on us, would you?"

Mrs. Irving laughed. "I assure you, I'm useless with

chemicals."

As I've said before, I'm a born people watcher. As a child in Hermann I was not popular among the other kids. I played, and had a small core of friends to be sure, but I now believe many of the other children were off put by my reading, by how well I did in school. Of course the usual divisions between Lutherans and Catholics played a part as well. So, often I spent my time watching people. I grew to notice small details of how we as a species interact—to better understand the unconscious vocabulary of gesture and expression.

So I watched the game. Mrs. Irving had a fine time playing with the four of us. She occasionally laid a hand on Daniel's arm or enjoyed a drink with Tom Bonehill, but she spent so much of the evening reading Samuel. I'm not sure anyone else might have noticed. It was a flicking of a gaze here, or a studied effort to stare from the corner of her eyes.

I wondered what had transpired between the two of them in that reading, weeks ago.

Bonehill rolled the whiskey in his glass. "What's your business, Mrs. Irving?"

"I'm here tending to my father's investments. He owns several hundred acres of ranch in Texas by the name of Pharoah's Point. Normally it is the work of a son, but as my father lacks such, I have come instead."

"Texas, really?" He raised his brows at that. Casually he leaned his chair back, fingering the visible sash at his waist. "I've just spent quite a bit of time there."

Her smile was coy. "I see the vaquero look about you, Señor Bonehill. Do not think I will be charmed witless by a killer."

The words brought to my mind the sight of a man sprawled beneath the pounding rain in the creep of wet earth and pooling blood, somewhere back in Nebraska. I looked away from Mrs. Irving, my eyes falling.

Bonehill did not flinch from the critique. his laugh was abrupt, two barks and a slap of the table. "You have my number, Mrs. Irving."

She tapped the table, and it was Daniel's turn. "Madame Irving, do you have much of an interest in the occult aside from the Tarot?"

The conversation receded into the back of my mind. I stared at my hands, my drink, the clock above the bar, Samuel. He seethed with pensive energy, often tapping his hand of cards harsh against the wood. Tak, tak. The cards audibly protested the treatment.

On either side of me, at the periphery of my attention, I vaguely registered the conversation taking a turn toward Mrs. Irving's pursuits of the occult—clubs her friends belonged to, books she had acquired, places she had been, and hobbies she had studied.

It sounded like the perfectly charmed existence of a bored dilettante at the time, but now I think my attitude was soured by our circumstances. In years since, she reaffirmed herself in my mind as a wonderful and charming woman, intelligent, and quick of wit.

The men, of course, were in love. It was written all over Bonehill's sly leer and constant offers to top off her glass. Likewise, it was painted all over Daniel's mooneyes and constant fumbling compliments. Samuel…Samuel I wasn't sure of. Often my attention drifted back to him. I wanted to know what he was thinking, what he was feeling. But he said nothing.

"You've an excellent face for poker, Mr. Clayton," Mrs. Irving said, snapping me out of my daze.

A voice spoke from behind us, drawing everyone's attention. "That's not his poker face, that's just Samuel."

85

I turned in my chair, hearing Bonehill curse beneath his breath. Barker Raleigh stood near, his stance loose, thumbs tucked in the suspenders beneath his clean dinner jacket. Nearby the man with the beastly right arm stood, hands on his hips, watching.

The reactions were as varied as the reactors. Daniel let slip a tiny querulous moan. Bonehill jumped to his feet. Samuel reached for a gun that was no longer there. His eyes rolled up, a silent curse at God for competent sheriffs.

The robber king held up his hands, an easy laugh rising from his lips. Casually, too casually, he pulled up a chair and joined us at the table. "I come in peace, gentlemen. I was sad things had to go the way they did last time we met. Deal me in?"

"If you think for one moment that we—" Daniel began, but was cut off at a gesture from Samuel.

My mentor, with all the cold composure he had to muster, collected the cards from the table and began to shuffle. Everyone remained silent, watching his long fingers work the cards. Aside from the occasional burp from the deck, our table was a void of quiescence in the starry sea of revelry around us. One by one Samuel flicked the cards to each of the participants—myself excluded of course—and tossed a pair of chips into the pot, signaling the game's start for the others.

It was Mrs. Irving that broke the frost. "So are none of you gentlemen going to introduce me to your handsome friend?"

"Their manners appear to have fled," Raleigh said with a slight flourish. "My deepest apologies. My friends call me Barker."

The distinctive name drew a flutter of uncertainty along Mrs. Irving's face. She glanced to the men on either side of her. Daniel focused singly on his cards while Bonehill chewed his cheek, glaring bullets at Raleigh.

Samuel drew a card from the deck and lay it down in the center of the table for all to see: A six of hearts. "What are you doing here, Raleigh?"

"I knew it!" Mrs. Irving cried. At startled looks from people at the other tables she sheepishly lowered her voice, leaning in. "You're him. You're Barker Raleigh, the famous bandit."

"The one and only." He tipped his hat. "My dear Samuel, I saw that you were in town and came to inquire what that episode in Nebraska was all about."

Mrs. Irving's eyes glittered. "Is it true? What they say about your fantastic treasure?"

He merely chuckled. As the saloon girl passed he flagged her down with a snap of his fingers. "Bourbon all around, darling. The good stuff—on me."

"It's true then," Mrs. Irving said.

"I'm not sure about fantastic treasure, but I've stored something back." He leaned in to give a conspiratorial wink. "I'm stockpiling for a rainy day."

"What day is that?" Samuel asked, finally looking up from his hand.

"A day of reckoning, my friend. A day of reckoning."

Daniel shook his head. "The war is over, Raleigh."

"Not for the righteous, it isn't." He thumped his chest. "The righteous will shake the pillars of this sinful nation and build a new world."

"The 'righteous' being you and thirty-some-odd thieves," Samuel said.

Raleigh smiled at that, a thin, smug curl of the lips. "My offer still stands, Samuel. We have a history, but there is no one on God's green earth I would rather stand shoulder to shoulder with. You're a good man—a *true* man. You still burn with a fury, I can see it in your face."

Samuel stared at the wall past me for the longest time, his eyes distant.

"The offer stands to present company as well, of course. We fought together. I'd have us reunited."

"All present company?" Mrs. Irving asked, not taking her eyes off her idling hand which played with a small stack of chips.

Raleigh gave an ingratiating smile. "Missus—"

"Irving," she said with silk smoothness. "Madeline Irving."

"Mrs. Irving, you may find our association a tad rough."

"Raise." Mrs. Irving's smile was crooked in more than one sense. She laid the stack of chips onto the pot. "A pity. Some girls will do anything for a little fun and fortune."

The men appraised their cards and one by one they folded—only Bonehill grumbled, and that seemed less for the lost bet than for the attention she lavished on the bandit. The deal fell to Daniel and he doled out the cards with a stubborn, forced cheerfulness.

"Nasty business, Brownville." Daniel tapped the edges of his cards against the table when all remaining had been dealt. He glanced up at Raleigh from beneath hooded eyes. "We witnessed what seemed to be a rather *withering* fire."

I saw then what he was doing. Raleigh ran a tongue over his teeth and said, "Yes. I seemed to have misplaced a pair of business associates. You haven't seen them, have you old boy?"

Samuel pushed his chair back from the table, reaching into his jacket. "Oh, for God's sake."

Men from all over the saloon stood as one and the room fell silent but for the click of a dozen or more hammers being drawn back. I looked around, astonished that Raleigh's men could have so filled the room without our noticing. Not everyone was a gang member, but there were enough present that we'd never have stood a chance—even armed.

Samuel's hand slid easily from the jacket, revealing his cigarillo case. Cautiously, wordlessly, he laid it on the table. "Just going for a smoke, Raleigh."

"Can't be too careful, old boy." The bandit hid a smile behind his bourbon glass. "Know you boys too well to think you'd be unarmed—even with a sheriff like Hickok."

I shifted uncomfortably, glad that he at least suspected we were armed. Perhaps that would give him pause if he decided to slaughter the lot of us. Nearby, one of his men got up and stood by the door, hand resting prominently on an old Griswold. Men who'd considered leaving sat back down, sullenly resuming their card games.

"Now we know the stakes," Raleigh said. He glanced around the table, eyes settling on me. He seemed to notice me for the first time. "Who's the pup, anyway?"

Bonehill opened his mouth but Samuel beat him. "A tag along. War orphan."

I felt my heart go leaden at the cold way he said the words. He took no notice of my hurt, holding his cigarillo to the lamp on the table and puffing until the end was glowing.

Raleigh's smile was a thoughtful one, calculated and cool. I was certain I'd just been sorted either into the 'expendable' stack, or the 'bargaining chip' stack. At last he turned his greasy gaze away from me, swatting at a fly that swooped near, and addressed the others.

"Where were we? Ah yes, lost business partners."

"Infernal things, those." Daniel's banter lacked some of its previous quiet self-satisfaction.

Raleigh looked at him, really looked at him, nodding slowly. "Yes, I suppose you know exactly what I mean." He looked about the table, nodding at each of the men. "Yes, I suppose most of you do."

89

I heard Mrs. Irving mutter, "I, for one, am utterly lost."

Raleigh continued, unfazed. "Should you run into my friend, let him know he has three days to show himself."

"Or else?" Bonehill asked.

"Or else someone's likely to get sacked." He gave his cards one more distasteful look and threw them face down on the table. Raleigh reached into a pocket and took out a fat handful of gold double-eagles. "I fold. Hope I gave you gentlemen something to think on."

Raleigh stood from the table and gave a tip of the hat and a wink for Mrs. Irving. "And you, ma'am. Have a pleasant evening."

Chapter Twelve

Bad Business

Nightmares dogged me.

Several times I woke up, sweating, pursued by visions of men with half-seen (or half missing?) faces, firing guns at me. At last I gave up on sleep and rolled out of bed.

"You can get some sleep, Samuel." I pulled my britches on and looped my braces over my shoulders. "I'll take over watch. Samuel?"

At the silence I turned to the window to find Samuel gone. The chair where he'd be sitting, keeping watch, was empty. No note, no sign of him.

Panicked, I searched the room, and my fears were confirmed. Samuel's possessions were gone. All that remained were my saddlebags with my change of clothes and my books. On the washstand I found the token for the livery where he'd stabled our horses.

Unbidden, unwanted, the worst conclusions began to formulate in my mind. I bolted from the room and began pounding on Bonehill and Daniel's door. I can only imagine what they found when they opened that door—a gasping, fretting boy on the edge of tears.

"Suh-Samuel!" I cried.

Bonehill pushed past me at once, a gun appearing in hand. He burst into our little room and scoped about.

"Where is he?" I heard him call.

"That—that's the problem." I clutched at my chest, my eyes beginning to burn. "S-suh-Samuel left me!"

It was admitting those words aloud that at last broke the damn. I collapsed against the wall, my eyes screwing up and my mouth forming an involuntary grimace. The tears came fast and hard.

Daniel, blurry eyed with interrupted sleep, pulled me into his room and Bonehill followed behind. Closing the door behind him, Bonehill pulled off his hat to scratch at his hair.

"God's blood, kid. What the hell is wrong with you? What do you mean Samuel left?"

"He left!" I wailed. It came out in one long trembling note. "He was waiting for the right offer and he took it and now he's gone!"

I felt an arm drape around me and I knew it to be Daniel's. I hid my tear-wet face in my hands and carried on for several minutes. The other two men, unsure, waited the storm out. Each time it seemed it was nearly over Bonehill would ask a question and that would cause the skies inside to begin thundering again.

"F-f-f-first my Papa died, and Samuel took me in and I thought everything was gonna be alright, and then he started being distant, and I knew it was coming but I didn't want to believe it, and now it's happened, and he's left me! He can't stand to take care of me be-because I'm not a good person and *why* did he leave me, Daniel? Why did he leave me?"

Daniel's flabbergasted voice came just to the side of me, and I looked up as he spoke. "I'm certain he's not left you, Charlie. He's fond of you—he made a promise to take care of you."

"Then where's he gone?" I asked, ashamed of the accusation in my voice. "Why was he chomping at the bits to run off and join a monster like Raleigh?"

Bonehill shook himself. "Raleigh? You think he went to Raleigh?"

I ran the length of my sleeve along my nose, leaving a snail trail. "Raleigh made him that offer in Brownville, 'member? He been looking for cause to ditch me since then."

The thought of the way he'd referred to me during the poker game came fresh to mind and I felt a knife twist in my heart. "A tag along. He never really wanted me. He just felt *sorry* for me."

"He's gone to Raleigh," Bonehill said to Daniel with a certainty as he slid his iron back into his slick Spanish holster. "I'm sure of it."

The other man shook his head, mouth working in silent disbelief. "He can't have betrayed us. I will not believe it."

"Truth don't need your belief, Daniel. You told me that too many times."

Daniel said nothing.

Bonehill looked on the verge of driving the point home when he was interrupted by a knock at the door. A moment later Mrs. Irving let herself in. The sole light was the moon, and the cream of her nightgown—of her skin—very nearly glowed. Her hair was let down, coming down to beneath her shoulder blades in long waves (100 strokes of the brush before bed, darling) and her eyes were as penetrating as a rail spike.

"I awoke to crying," she said. "Is it Charlie? What is the matter?"

At once she crossed the room to me and knelt, a finger tracing the wet tear track on my cheek. Mrs. Irving stared at me a long time and finally embraced me. Not knowing what else to do, feeling like a castoff and adrift, I put my arms around her neck and hugged her tight. When I felt my chest beginning to bubble with more morose sobs I heard the strangest thing.

I heard her sing.

I don't know if she ever sang for you, Amelia. It's not something she did often, and I cannot say that she had a

93

lovely singing voice. But it was an honest voice, and full of care and affection. Later, she would tell me it was a song her Scottish nanny used to sing to her. She sang:

Can ye not hush your weeping
A' the wee babies are sleeping
Birdies are nestling, and nestling together
But my bonnie baby is waking yet

Dreams to sell, fine dreams to sell,
Angus is here with dreams to sell o
Hush my wee baby and sleep without fear
Dream Angus has brought you a dream my dear

Hear the curlew crying o
And the echoes dying o
Even the birdies are cuddled up sleeping
But my bonnie baby is weeping greeting

Dreams to sell, fine dreams to sell,
Angus is here with dreams to sell o
Hush my wee baby and sleep without fear
Dream Angus has brought you a dream my dear

Soon the lavrock sings his song
Welcoming the coming dawn
Lambies come down the gather
With the yowies in the heather

Dreams to sell, fine dreams to sell,
Angus is here with dreams to sell o
Hush my wee baby and sleep without fear
Dream Angus has brought you a dream my dear

At the end, the room was quiet. Bonehill's bluster was gone, Daniel's denials. The fire of my sorrow, of my loss was now merely banked coals. They burned there, deep, but they would not consume me for now.

"That was lovely, Mrs. Irving," Daniel said after a moment.

She did not look at him, still holding me. "I like you gents, and I'm fond of Charlie. You should know that I am not married—but I know society frowns on an unattached woman wandering about. You may call me Maddy, as my friends do."

Maddy—she pulled away to look at me. She stroked my hair into shape and finally stood up.

"Gentlemen, I am going to wake Graham and then I will get dressed. When I am ready we're going to search for your Samuel. Do you have any good ideas of where to start?"

The two hunters glanced at one another, and gave a nod.

"You and I," Daniel said. "We're thinking the same."

Bonehill stroked his pointed beard. "I bet some of Raleigh's boys are still drinkin' down at the Beaver."

I spoke up, my voice feeling swollen and thick. "Raleigh's jacket was clean."

"What?" Bonehill asked.

"It was clean. No road dust. He was also shaved. I think he's staying somewhere local."

He stared at me for a long moment, seeing me in a fresh light. Later, Tom Bonehill would tell me that he always ignored my deductions because he assumed Samuel always fed me hints. Without Samuel to help, however, there could be no other explanation save that I had arrived at the deductions of my own accord.

"Then we shall go to the Blue Beaver," Maddy said. "Let us retrieve our weapons from Sheriff Hickok. Come, quickly."

95

It was given to Bonehill to sneak a peek. He slunk up the boardwalk leading to the windows of the saloon, and I was amazed at how quiet he walked. Any other man would have clomped on those boards, would have jangled with those spurs. But he moved like a puma through the oil lamp darkness and sidled casually by the window.

He took two glances, too calm to be obviously spying, then wandered our way. As soon as he was in the dust of the alley way he herded us deeper into the shadows.

"Four boys left I recognized from earlier. Something strange, though."

"What?" Daniel asked.

He shook his head, as if not believing himself. "Thought I caught a glimpse of one in the mirror over the bar and—well." Bonehill steeled himself. "It's probably nothing."

"Nothing, given what we do?" I asked. I stood apart from the other three, holding the reins of the horses.

Maddy looked between the two hunters and myself, tapping her lips. "What is it exactly that you gentlemen do again?"

"Bounty hunters," Daniel said too fast.

"Mm," was her only reply. Graham grunted beside her, implacable.

"The mirror," Bonehill said. "They didn't look quite right in the mirror, but I couldn't get a good eye on 'em in the time I was up there."

"Can you get another look?" Maddy asked.

He looked around at the lot of us and gave a curt bob of the head. He was at the mouth of the alley when he froze. A moment later he slunk back into the shadows as four shapes sauntered past. The boys were hooting and howling, drunk on whiskey and the fat of life. One was blatantly showing off his six-gun, waving it in the air, miming the action of shooting people in the street and out of windows.

"If those fools get arrested before we can follow 'em…" I heard Bonehill mutter. He leaned out as they walked past and after a brief moment he waved us forward. Maddy and Daniel took their reins and started off. I mounted up and led Bonehill's rangy horse to him. The creature was all legs, looking like he'd be good over sand and rock, but maybe not so great for distance at speed.

We followed at a distance, but it was hard to seem innocuous at a time of night when so few were on the streets. Luckily we were helped by the occasional wandering cowboy off spending his pay in Abilene's saloons and whorehouses. The four of us had to guide our horses on to a side street when the boys stopped to collect theirs from a hitching post. They did not seem to notice us when we came out three streets down, following them again.

Bonehill rode ahead of us, scouting the way through the darkened Abilene streets. We rode slowly, casually, waiting for a signal from him to turn a corner and follow. The Raleigh boys had two hundred, three hundred yards on us when we left town at its southern edge and came out onto the lonely Kansas prairie. But if they heard us, there was no sign. Even in the dark we could follow them by the glow of their cigarettes and the loud, bawdy songs they sang.

I think we must have ridden three or four miles when the lights of a homestead appeared in the darkness. Yellow lamplight shone in windows. When the Raleigh boys vanished inside all we were left with was the sound of coyotes and night birds.

We hitched the horses in a copse near the homestead, everyone drawing their instruments. I checked that my Sharps was loaded and that my holster was secure at my hip. To my right I saw Daniel patting his pocket nervously for his pistol.

To my left Bonehill drew that impressive leather case from off the back of his saddle. The idea of seeing it in action made my mouth water, despite my fears.

But before we began the walk toward the house Bonehill laid a hand on Maddy's arm. "I think you should stay with the horses."

"And I think you should mind your own business." She jerked her arm free and drew a handsomely etched Henry rifle from her saddle scabbard, reflecting bright moonlight in its polished fittings. "I can handle myself. And if I stay, Graham stays—and I believe you will desire his assistance, am I correct?"

Graham nodded. "Most accurate, ma'am."

She drew imperiousness about her like a protective cloak. "Graham is not merely a butler, but a veteran soldier. Is that not correct, Graham?"

"Right again, ma'am. Ten years in His Majesty's service."

Even in the dark I could still see Bonehill's frown, but he said nothing else on the matter.

We each moved as silently as we could through the knee-high grass. Daniel and Bonehill, veterans both, had skill born of hard times. I had what Samuel had managed to teach me over the last year we'd been together. Maddy and Graham were surprisingly quiet, Maddy slinking along with only a whisper of cloth despite both the dress and the bustle. Still, such a large group together makes noise, so we moved at a tortoise pace.

At a hundred and fifty yards out we reached a wooden fence, the timber fresh cut and yellow. Bonehill ordered everyone to the grass. The black leather case lay before him. He muffled the sounds of the clasps with his fingers and took the Whitworth out with a kind of quiet reverence.

He cared for that rifle, operated it with a kind of religious awe. Complete silence fell over our group, sans even the sound of our breath. The case held slots for ten bullets, four of which were vacant—five now. The paper cartridge slid into the banded barrel and tamped down with the rod. The cap slipped into place beneath the hammer which was drawn back so slow I could almost imagine Bonehill's thumb knuckle creaking.

Finally he adjusted his hooded sight and peered through it. As one the four of us gazed at the homestead. A lamp burned on the porch and at the windows, casting place in ominous light, and I could see figures moving beyond. The windows themselves were oilcloth, not glass. The wood was new, but thin, and only a lean-to shelter on the side served for the lone horse and cow. It was the homestead of someone new to town and without much money.

The boys we'd followed were already inside, and on the breeze I could just make out the sound of folk arguing. Someone was shouting someone else down, and then came the distant chiming tinkle of glass breaking. A bottle, perhaps?

"There," Daniel whispered. He pointed to a shadow rising up out of the yard opposite us. Bonehill quickly placed the figure under his sights, trying to get a better look.

The figure stood just beyond the light—and it called, "Raleigh!"

I said it as soon as I realized what I was seeing.

"Samuel—!"

"The whoreson did it. He betrayed us," Bonehill said, still peering through his sights. He seemed to be lining Samuel up.

The house fell silent. Shapes appeared at the windows, moving their cloth aside.

The door cracked, swung wide. Barker Raleigh stood in his shirt and suspenders, gun slung low over his hip. "That you, old boy? That really you?"

"It's really me, Barker." Samuel reached slowly into his pocket and the wind carried the sound of a dozen hammers drawing back. He spoke clearly, raising his voice only enough to be heard across the distance. "Easy, easy. I bring a peace offering."

The hand slipped out of his pocket holding something glittering in the wan light.

The coin.

Even at a hundred and fifty yards, I could feel the hunger radiating off of Raleigh. One hand rested at his chest, twitching—either toward his gun or his breast pocket. "Wonderful, old boy, wonderful. Welcome to the fold. Quick, come into the warmth and bring it here."

Samuel took two steps forward and a wolf's grin formed on Raleigh's lips. But Samuel stopped just shy of the light. "I got questions first."

"And you shall have answers in time."

The hand holding the coin lowered to his side. Slowly, he shook his head. "Need to know—first. This coin, Raleigh. Know what it is. I worry you're involved in bad business."

In the clear night air, under that big Kansas sky, their voices carried to us as if they were across an empty room.

"The Samuel Henry Clayton I knew was not a superstitious man. He brooked no nonsense."

"Ain't superstition, Raleigh. It's fact. You've made some bad friends."

Raleigh's hand twitched again. I thought I felt a building energy, like the air before a thunderstorm. "Just pass me the coin, Sammy. I done all for the greater good, and you'll see that—in time."

I saw Samuel's shoulders slump, saw his hands rolling the coin around in his fingers. After a moment's hesitation he nodded.

"He's going to do it," Bonehill breathed beside me.

A sharp pain caused me to suddenly realize I'd been biting my lip to bleeding. I felt Maddy's hand on my shoulder. More for myself than the others I said, "No, he won't. He can't."

"More faith'n you gave him a few hours ago." Bonehill adjusted himself, the Whitworth bearing down on Samuel.

"No," I said, worried I'd said it too loud. I lowered my voice. "No, aim for Raleigh."

The look he gave me could smelt iron. Reluctantly he turned back to his sights and shifted the rifle lining up on the robber king. One hand absently reached up to tilt the brim of his Mexican hat back. He breathed in.

The moment to fire never came.

Samuel tossed the coin across the void of the night. As Raleigh's left hand reached out to catch it his right hand came up blazing lead. Shots rang out—one, two. No, three. But I'd only seen Raleigh's gun fire twice.

Samuel stood there in the dark yard, in the cattle-cropped grass, the Remington already smoking in his hands. He'd fired first. He'd meant to fire all along.

Raleigh stumbled, missed the coin. He looked around, bewildered at the world around him. Bewildered by Samuel, bewildered by his men. His left hand, empty, rose to his neck and as I watched black began to leak from between his fingers. He dropped to the boards of the porch with a loud plunk.

I exhaled. I almost cheered. But Maddy's hand shook my shoulder and I looked at Samuel. He took one step, two, then fell to his face in the grass.

"Samuel!" I cried. "Samuel, no!"

Two of Raleigh's men burst out of the door, one trying to reclaim their boss and the other darting through the dark toward Samuel. The air cracked like ice and he fell to Tom Bonehill's Whitworth.

"There's more of 'um out here," someone shouted. "Get the boss! Open fire boys! *Fire!*"

The night air lit with the sounds of scattered pistol fire. Overhead I heard the angry wasp buzz of bullets flying over our general direction.

"Samuel," I said, trying to stand. "Someone needs to get Samuel!"

"Get down!" Daniel said, dragging me back to the grass. "You'll lose your head!"

Beside me, Bonehill was already tamping down another cartridge into the Whitworth and on the other side of me Maddy and Graham had begun giving lead to the people in the house.

Men did not fall under the fire—it was quite a distance for us—but they were less likely to begin charging us while Bonehill reloaded. Points of light flickered in the darkness where her lead punched holes in the wood of the little house. And inside I heard something suddenly.

Screaming.

I strained to listen. There was of course the angry shouts of the hive of robbers that we'd kicked, but underneath that was the high keening sound of someone else.

"There's kids in there."

Chapter Thirteen

October Rain

I turned on Bonehill. "What if they're holding a family hostage?"

"Not a lot we can do about that now." The hunter was lining up his sights on the shadow of a head appearing at the window. The Whitworth flashed and I heard the distant wail of a man shot.

"We gotta get to Samuel." He immediately began clearing the barrel and preparing a fresh cartridge.

Daniel looked round the three of us and swallowed. "I'll do it. I'll go. No—Charlie, don't give me that look. You couldn't hope to carry him back. You're too little."

To my dismay Maddy nodded agreement. "He's right, young Charlie. Mister Garner, I'll join you. You need someone to discourage those men from putting holes in you."

"Are you any good with that?" Daniel glanced at the Henry in her hands. The fine etching on the brass, the delicate carving on the stock said more about her money than it did about her skill.

"I've months of practice with coyotes on the trail," she said as she began to slot new brass cartridges into the breech. "Four legs or two, a coyote's a coyote."

Beside her, Graham laid his hat on the ground and drew his Colt, nodding agreement.

A moment later Bonehill lined up a fresh victim and felled him. The Raleigh gang was hurt by the dark—we could see them a hell of a lot better than they could see us. Three or four men down at his hands, the gang was more cautious now. Return fire came less erratically now. They were biding their time, likely watching the spot where Samuel lay.

"On the count of three," Maddy said, and Bonehill nodded.

"One."

"Two."

"Three."

The two of them stood as one and leapt the fence. The skirt of her dress caught on the wood, but she kept running, giving it a hard yank. It tore free, exposing a white flash of her petticoat. She paid no heed. As figures began to rise in the door and windows she opened up on them, sending them back to cover.

Meanwhile Bonehill frowned down at his rifle. "I've got one left, and we may still need it. Give me the Sharps."

"But—"

"I'm a better shot than you, kid. Good, thank you. And the cartridges in your pocket."

With a soldier's efficiency he took the Sharps, lined up on the sight, and squeezed off a dose of lightning in the direction of the house. Another body fell as Daniel and Maddy reached Samuel and I felt myself seethe with vindication. That sense of black triumph ended only a moment later when the screaming of the children came back worse than before.

"Fire!" someone shouted in the house.

"…knocked over a lamp!"

"Put out the damn fire!"

Beside me Bonehill's face went ashen. "Jerusalem crickets! Alright, Charlie. Now's your chance."

"But…"

"No, buts! You wanted to go save those girls? Do it now."

At his word I rose and started toward the back of the house. I wasn't sure what I was going to do, but I had to figure it out quickly. I crouch-ran through the tall grass, trying to find a back way in, but I was so focused on the house that I didn't see another shape rise out of the dark.

I don't know who was more surprised—the bandit or I. We stared at each other for the space of several heartbeats trying to figure out what we were looking at. He must have come from the back of the house to try to flank us. He went for his gun first.

I screamed, my voice cracking with rage and panic, and bowled into him headfirst. We fell to the ground and I heard the sound of air evacuate his lungs, and the crack of his pistol firing wide.

We rolled there in the dirt for several moments and he nearly had me. He grabbed one wrist, pinning me, then reached for the other. I was too fast for him, too fast for even myself. Without realizing what I was doing I drew the knife at his belt and plunged it into his gut.

He froze, dazed surprised. It was enough for me. I broke away, kicking his pistol from his hand where it lay on the ground. The hilt of the knife stood upright in his belly like a grave marker, and he stared at me as I first backed away and then ran.

I was fully automatic now, unthinking—just a train running its track. How could I think? I'd spent weeks castigating myself for taking a life, and now I'd taken another.

My feet carried me around the back of the house. There was a small yard fenced in with wire. A chicken coop nearby clucked madly with disturbed hens. And there, I saw what I needed. A door hung open on heavy leather hinges, sending a long ray of light across the yard. Inside it was worse than I thought. I could see smoke pouring through the door, and one inner wall was aflame. The new wood was catching too quickly.

But the men? Where were the men?

"Find the girl," someone shouted.

105

Another replied, "I can't see her. I think she locked 'erself in the bedroom again."

"Then leave her to burn! We still got the others."

Three men fled out the open front door, where I saw a crowd of the remaining Raleigh gang. We were far outnumbered.

But then there *was* still a girl in the house.

I pulled my shirt up over my mouth and stormed inside, looking around. The house was shot to hell, the meager belongings disturbed by our lead thunderstorm. Some distant, still conscious part of me recognized the lack of dead bodies in the room and thought it strange. The locomotive, however, ran to the door along the burning wall.

"Help me! Help!" a voice screamed from the other side, shrill. She began to cough. "Somebody, please!"

I grabbed the wrought iron doorknob, unthinking of the heat, and yanked. The door rattled in its frame but did not open. The knob and lock had to be the nicest thing in this house, and now it had trapped a girl inside.

My presence must have drawn the attention of the girl on the other side. In an instant there was pounding on the wood, muffled pleas for help.

I backed up three steps and charged the door. The shock rattled my brain inside my skull, but hardly the door. Three steps back again, and this time I felt the blow begin to ache in my shoulder. But still the door wouldn't budge. My lungs burned with a need to cough.

I darted a nervous glance outside after I'd recovered, doubled over with coughing. I couldn't hear what was going on outside over the fire, and apparently no one had noticed me yet. My lungs were wracked with another fit.

I tried to shout, "Back away from the door!" but the smoke burned. The best I could manage was "Back!"

I drew my gun and shot the lock. The door swung outward under the weight of a girl and bowled me to the ground. A moment later she toppled onto me.

She was a filthy urchin of a girl with soot stained hair the color of fall in glory, and wearing boy's britches and braces. We stared at one another for a heartbeat before we both scrambled to rise and escape the burning house.

The creak of a floorboard behind us was all the warning I got of what came next.

As I spun to look one of Raleigh's men had come back in and was pulling his revolver from his pocket. The hammer must have snagged on a seam. I had enough time to retrieve my own from the floor.

Out of the corner of my eye I saw the man standing upright in a mirror. The arm, my God, it was the man with the massive right hand. The scrape of leather drew my attention to the cavalry saber he was drawing from its scabbard.

His reflection did not bear the same visage as what I saw before me. It was shrunken, desiccated, buzzing with flies and crawling with maggots. The man's eyes had grown cloudy and white with rot, and black fluid dribbled from his mouth and down his bib shirt.

I saw all this in the flash of a second but there was no time to think on what it was. As I leveled on him he raised his saber. The Dance roared, rattling the walls and sending me reeling backward.

The sword flashed downward and my chest flared with fire. Momentum carried me back against the jamb and when I opened my eyes I found my shirt torn open and a line of red across my chest.

Across from me, the misshapen bandit looked at his own chest. A hole opened up on his breast, oozing blackness. He seemed too stunned to raise the sword again.

Thus the girl and I fled from the doomed house.

Out in the cool air, beyond the chickens and the little yard, we collapsed in the shadows of the tall grass and spent several minutes sucking the cool, fresh air. When our hacking and gasping finally subsided she jumped to her feet and began screaming.

"My Da! My brothers!"

"No, no, no," I said, trying to shush her. "Quiet. Please. You'll draw their attention."

"Da! Daddy!" Tears began to run down her cheeks, clearing away the black gauze of soot. She ran through the grass, back toward the house, silhouetted against the bright blaze of the house.

"They weren't in the house," I called after her. After another moment of caught breath I clumsily shoved my Dance into my holster and chased after her.

We ran, through the grass, past a dark patch of blood where a body should have been. She ran for the front and I, helpless, chased after her. We had nearly rounded the corner when the air split with the sound of two more gunshots. And then a third.

"*No!*"

The girl hurled herself toward the yard in time to see war erupt anew. In time to see Raleigh's men retreating into the dark beyond the light of the house's inferno. In time to see Maddy at last drag Samuel's limp body to safety.

In time to see a grown man and two small boys collapse, sacrificial goats to ensure the retreat of the Raleigh gang.

The girl screamed, as loud and heartbreaking a noise as I'd ever heard come from a human mouth. It was fury and anguish together. It was wrath.

She snatched a knife discarded on the ground and charged after the retreating gang. It was only my quick thinking that saved her from the same fate that took her family. I bore her to the ground and endured her kicks, her punches, and her attempts to stab me.

Her struggle lasted a long time, long after the hail of lead over us silenced. At last she settled, her eyes glazing over. Tears rushed over her face, quiet and hopeless, cleansing the last of the soot.

Chapter Fourteen

Silver Reveals

Maddy knew a doctor by the name of Thackery in Abilene. We rushed our horses as best we could with a man unconscious from blood loss. Soon Bonehill was pounding down the doctor's door, waking him and several of his neighbors.

Doctor Thackery's face settled into something more than a little judgmental when he saw our state, saw Samuel, but he said nothing. He was discreet and efficient. He tried to shoo me from Samuel's side, and eventually it took Bonehill and Daniel, both, to remove me. The girl almost seemed to be waiting for me on the street outside when I was dragged out, kicking and yelling.

The two Brothers remained inside to help in any way they could, including holding Samuel down. Locked out of the building, all I could do was watch empty windows and listen to the sound of Samuel screaming.

After an eternity Samuel's hollering subsided and Bonehill came out to join the womenfolk and I. He scrubbed his hands on a towel lent by Doctor Thackery, clearing away the blood.

"The doctor didn't need you nipping at his heels, boy," he said, not unkindly. He wouldn't even look in the girl's direction.

She rubbed at her puffy eye, sniffled miserably. "That man was your da, yeah?"

I chewed my lip, looked away from her. I couldn't bear to look her in the eye—couldn't bear the idea of seeing yet more pity direct toward me. But rather than pity I felt her hand reach out, her fingers tangling with mine, and squeeze tight.

"I hope he's alright," she said, her voice lilting with a heavy Irish brogue. "You're the boy from the train, ain't ya—the one what wore a gun? We met when Da was taking us out here."

I faltered. "You're…"

"October. Da calls—called me Toby." She sniffled again, her eyes darting about uncertainly.

"Toby…" I looked at the others around me. Daniel nodded encouragingly and Maddy gave a small, sad smile. Bonehill was sunk into his own thoughts. "Toby, I'm sorry about your family."

I feared I'd said the wrong thing. The corners of her mouth wrenched down and she screwed up her eyes. She made a thin, high sound that turned into a full-throated wail. The word 'Bereaved' was coined to describe the noise she made in that moment, reaved of her kin.

I was lost, unsure of what to do, until I saw a small gesture from Maddy. At her insistence, I put my arms around Toby's scrawny shoulders and held onto her tight while she sobbed out her fears and her loss.

Doctor Thackery and Daniel found us just after dawn. We sat on the edge of the boardwalk sipping coffee out of tin cups. Toby slept against Bonehill's shoulder and he sat, stiff-jawed, too scared to move.

Peering at us in the daylight the Doctor would have seen a shabby bunch. A boy, an Irish girl, a high-class lady, and a desperado. Toby and I were filthy with soot and dirt, while Maddy's nice dress and Bonehill's jacket were smeared with fresh streaks of mud and bodily fluids. I think if you were to look at me then, you would have seen a gaunt and lost gaze, hopeless.

It is for that reason perhaps that Doctor Thackery seemed

to address me when he spoke. "It's not so bad as it could have been. I believe your man was already running exhausted to begin with and might have collapsed anyway. The bullets will do him no good, but I see that he is no stranger to trouble."

He gave us all a significant look at that.

"One bullet shattered his left arm, four inches above the elbow. He'll be in a sling for a while. The other passed through the meat around his abdomen. Inch in any direction and the shot would have been fatal. He's very lucky. Give him lots of rest and good meat. He needs to recover lost blood."

Samuel spent the rest of the day and the next night at the doctor's sleeping. I stayed by his side, frequently visited by the others. In the times when we were alone, though, I stared at his bedside and talked.

"Thought I'd lost you," I said once, mid morning. He was in the deep, quiet still of sleep.

"It was like losing my pa all over again." I hung my head. It ached from fear, throbbed from hours of crying. "Why did you do it, Samuel? Why?"

For the thousandth time I played the events of the night out in my head, imagining every moment in vivid detail. It is a natural human reaction to begin making excuses for the strange and the unnatural, and a scab of uncertainty was already starting to form over the memories of what I'd seen there in the mirror of that burning house.

But I was familiar with that scab and how to pick at it. I pulled and peeled, trying to balm the strangeness with logic and reason without quite realizing what I was doing.

What I'd seen in the mirror was a walking corpse, quite unlike the man I'd shot. Now, I thought to myself, I'd seen somewhere in the Charlotte Bible that silver had a purifying effect on certain black powers, negating them or cleansing them. Could I see something in a silvered mirror that I might not see with my own eyes?

And then there were the other inconsistencies. Had it been my imagination, or were bodies disappearing? If Raleigh had been shot dead (and what else could a hole in the neck be, if not fatal?) then why were his men so eager to retrieve him? Where was the fellow I'd stabbed in the yard? For that matter where were any of the bodies of the men Tom Bonehill had sniped?

Two images fluttered there in my consciousness: My Dance revolver recoiling in my hand as I shot down a man in a little back alley in Brownville, and the sight of that same man hanging dead from a tree miles away. I wondered how that could be, why it would be necessary to hang a man who was shot dead.

It was the image in the mirror.

"They're dead men walking!" I said, hearing a startled grunt from Doctor Thackery in the other room.

Of course. They could not be killed because somehow, some *way* they were already dead. Mirrors, silver, could reveal the truth of it.

"Samuel, I have it! I need to tell the others."

Breathless, I ran from the recovery room. Rounding the corner to the entry hall I collided into a body and nearly reeled backwards. Firm hands caught me and I looked up. Maddy held me tight, a corner of her mouth quirked up in a confused smile.

"Easy there, Charlie. Where are ye running off too? Has Samuel awoken?"

"Not yet, but I think I figured out the Ra—" I glanced at the doctor's drawing room where I saw him watching us over the rims of his spectacles. "I think I've figured out what we're dealing with."

"Goodness, I'd love to hear it."

"I'll tell you when I get back. I need to tell Daniel and Bonehill."

"They're at the Beaver now."

She shooed me off with a smile, claiming the noise wasn't good for Samuel's recovery.

The Blue Beaver at midday, while not abandoned, gave off the impression of being empty. Perhaps five of the fifteen tables had occupants, and none were full save one—ours. There was no haze of tobacco smoke fogging up the air, and the pianist had taken time away from his ill-tuned instrument to flirt with the girl sweeping the floors.

As I said before, I spied the Charlottes as soon as I walked in. Refusing to be snuck up upon again, Daniel and Bonehill had taken a table in the far corner of the establishment where they could drink and talk in peace. Unfortunately this meant that when Bill Hickok had come for them, they saw him stare them down the whole way back.

The legendary sheriff spared me a glance, sizing me up in a moment before turning back on them. It seemed the three of them were embroiled in a heated conversation. Daniel's books lay open and unread while their beers were half-drunk and abandoned.

"Gentlemen," Hickok said with a warning tone. "Pray tell, do tell me again how it is that you did not think Barker Raleigh and his boys were in Abilene?"

Bonehill's long, shootist's fingers drummed the top of the table. "Gladly, Sheriff Hickok. I will tell you once more that we found no sign that Raleigh had abandoned the tracks to veer off in a different direction. For all we knew, he and his men was using the rail to hide their movements. We were in sore need of a rest, and thus…"

He made a broad gesture his arms, encompassing the whole of Abilene and the events contained within.

114

"And for the record," My hero lazily pulled the makings of a cigarette from his coat's pocket. "Why is it exactly that you did not come and immediately report to me when he made his presence known? That he was armed within city limits? How is it that I was only to learn of these events when I investigated what sounded a *hell* of a lot like a gunfight? I found a burned out homestead not three miles from town and the bodies of a man and *two little boys!*"

"Sir, we did not think," Daniel began before Hickok shouted him down.

"You did not think perhaps that the law took greater precedence over your personal profit?" He was quivering, purple rage now. Spit flew from beneath his handlebar mustache, hitting Daniel (and making him more than a little uncomfortable).

Of course neither of them would tell *the* Wild Bill Hickok that it was personal. Neither of them would tell *the* Wild Bill Hickok that they didn't think he could take on a man bargaining with some kind of devil.

The devil—the coin! Of course!

Without knowing it, I danced on the balls of my feet behind Wild Bill, anxious to talk to Daniel. Wild Bill turned around in his seat, his rage melting.

He popped off his hat and smoothed back his long ringlets of hair. "Why hello, boy. Needing an autograph?"

That stopped my fidgeting.

I supposed it couldn't hurt. "If—if I may, sir."

"But of course!" He extended his hand for the object to be signed.

My hands searched the pockets of my britches, my outer jacket pockets, and then the pocket inside. And there, the little copy of *On a Springfield Evening*. I must have rolled it away and tucked it there for further reading at some point recently. I

115

pulled it out and passed it to him.

He looked over the book, flipping through it. At a couple choice passages he chuckled to himself. "Just a moment, son. Need to find m'self a pen."

He looked around, eyes settling on Daniel's stack of books and the sturdy tin bottle of ink and the pen he was using to take notes. "May I?"

Daniel stuttered, flustered, but agreed. He slid the bottle and pen to Wild Bill.

"To whom shall I dedicate?"

"Charlie, sir," I said, a nervous edge creeping into my voice. "Charlie Kirchner."

Wild Bill inked the pen and signed my book with a great flourish. "Cherish it," Wild Bill said proudly, patting me on the shoulder.

He passed the book back to me and gave me another look-over. "That's a fine neck tie you have, Charlie Kirchner. You keep it up, you may dress as dandy as I do one day."

I beamed.

"Now if you'll excuse me, I have business with these good-for-nothings here." He gestured to Daniel and Bonehill.

"Actually so do I, sir."

Wild Bill took another look at me, seeing me—really seeing me—for the first time. "Ah, you're the boy who was traveling with them before. I suppose you do, then. Still, wouldn't do for you to be here right now. Hate for you to see me tear these gentlemen a new asshole."

I took a deep breath, screwing up my courage. "I—I really need to talk to them, sir."

He narrowed his eyes. Though I'd changed, I hadn't washed after my encounter. He looked at my hands, seeing the marks of gunpowder there. I could tell he knew in that moment I'd been present with the others last night.

"Dangerous business, boy. Is this about Barker Raleigh?"

"It's about Samuel," I lied.

He narrowed his eyes. "Samuel, being…?"

"He's part of our group."

Everyone looked at me expectantly, but I said nothing. I studied the floorboards and my feet intensely, not standing up to everyone's scrutiny. Apparently I could stare down an eviscerating horror, but not the stern gazes of my heroes.

Wild Bill cleared his throat. "Gentlemen, I'll leave you now. If you decide you have anything to tell me," he said through his teeth, "You'll know where to find me."

He excused himself, leaving the saloon with one hand resting comfortably on a cross-draw pistol and the other holding up his burning cigarette for inspection. The other men in the room stared openly at us after he was gone, shocked that we had survived the wrath of Wild Bill Hickok. Daniel and I had the good sense to look sheepish about the episode, but Bonehill startled the men into minding their own damned business with a fierce glare.

I made myself comfortable at the table and told them everything, leaning in and speaking in quiet hushed tones. When I finished Daniel made me walk through my reasoning: The corpse in the mirror, the missing bodies, the urgency to retrieve Raleigh's cadaver, and lastly the coin.

"This explains why those folk were so certain they'd killed him," Bonehill said into his beer mug as he lifted it to his lips. By the end of my story he'd been nodding along.

Daniel frowned to himself. "And why he'd been so eager to get the coin back."

"If you'd struck a deal with a devil, you'd be eager to hang on to his cat house token, too," Bonehill said.

That caused Daniel to sit up straight. "Of course!"

"Of course?" I asked.

Already he was fishing through the books laid out on the table. He pulled out his Bible and started flipping pages until he settled on one thick with fresh notes. There on the page were charcoal impressions of the two sides of the coin. He read it off "He so calls me, calls me Wither. The coin wasn't only being used to hide his presence from the law, this Wither was giving them effective immortality."

"Do you think Samuel knew?" Bonehill stared into his beer.

Daniel shrugged uncomfortably. "He might've. Keeps his cards awful close to his chest."

"I suppose we won't be able to ask for awhile," I said.

"How is he?" Daniel asked.

"Still sleeping." I stared down at my powder stained hands. "Where's Toby?"

"Sleeping at the hotel," Bonehill said. "Girl's plum tuckered."

Daniel saw that I was fed, commenting that it wouldn't do to starve myself for Samuel's sake. When I parted ways with the other Charlotte brothers I walked back to the doctor's office. I could hear the shouting even before I opened the door.

"The hell do you even care for?" The voice was Samuel's, though froggy and raw.

I opened the door, peering down the hallway which bisected the building from the front door to the back. The parlor to my right served as the doctor's office. Rooms running down the left side served as examination and operating rooms.

"I care because I care, you damnable stubborn ox." And that was certainly Maddy's voice. The shouting match was coming from Samuel's room.

I crept there, glancing in the parlor as I passed—apparently

Doctor Thackery had stepped out. A mirror opposite the door to Samuel's room revealed the truth. They were shouting, but they were close—terribly close. He had her gripped by the cloth of her shoulder and her arms were placed to either side of his neck where he reclined in bed.

"You're just here for the gold," I heard him say in a dangerously low voice.

She sniffed indignantly, pulling away from him. "That's a filthy accusation. I'm here because the cards said I would be here."

"Fate." Samuel snorted. "Right. Get out."

"I will!"

"And don't come back!"

She drew herself upright, taking the bearing of a queen. "Mister Clayton, if my presence is a thorn in your comfort I will be sure to make myself known to you every last day you draw breath."

As I neared the open door to the room Maddy came bustling out, skirts hiked up and out of her way. Her face was flustered and her hair out of place. And I noticed the first three buttons of her dress' high neck were unfastened.

She stopped when she saw me, a fresh red flush coming to her face. Fastening her buttons she stammered for a moment. Finally gathering her composure, Maddy caressed my cheek fondly and said, "You've the patience of all the saints for putting up with that...that *man*."

I lost my voice at the touch, fumbling for a brief moment. Again she smiled for me and excused herself out of the office. She slammed the door for good measure, hard enough to cause the trim windows on either side of it to rattle in their casings.

Chapter Fifteen

Innocence and Vigor

I turned on my heels and followed her out the door. "Miss
Maddy! Miss Maddy."

She stopped, turning and waiting for me. Her smile was
tired and forced. At the time I thought she was covering up for
her anger but now I know better—I'll talk about that soon.
Maddy tucked a stray curl of hair behind her ear, trying to set
her tousled bun right.

"Charlie, I'm sorry you had to see that," she said as I
caught up.

"What was it? Why were you fighting?"

She took a deep breath. Her hands fidgeted nervously.
"Charlie—your first reading. I told you I'd seen a dark
shadow in your presence and future, yes?"

I nodded. "Yes. I think I know what it is."

"At the time I thought I knew what it was, as well. Samuel."

I almost laughed. "Samuel? Maddy, he's—he's saved my
life. He looks after me, teaches me. He's my friend."

She shook her head, looking away. "I felt something black
in him. The cards did as well. And they said other things."
She seemed to consider telling me what those other things
were but changed tack. "There are many ways the cards can
be interpreted. I think I did so wrongly. Time is starting to
show me their meaning."

I noticed the faint blush rising on her cheeks.

"What do you…"

Maddy fixed me with an enigmatic smile. "A good reader
never tells another soul's fortune, darling. I'm famished.
Pardon, I'm going to fetch Graham and have him fetch

some—what do you call them? Ah, vittles."

And she was gone. I scratched my head, watching her sashay off.

"Hell of a woman," someone nearby said. I was inclined to agree.

Back in the office Samuel was sitting up trying to pull the cork from a bottle of Old Crow with only one hand.

"What are you doing?" I asked.

"Hurts to beat the devil."

"Give me that," I said, swiping the bottle from his hand. He made a noise of protest but I popped the cork and poured a finger into a tin cup at his bedside.

We sat in silence for a long while. He stared into his cup long after he'd emptied it, not looking at me. His beard had grown wild over the months of our chase and his hair was matted and flat on one side from sleep. His eyes were bloodshot and I thought I could see signs of his crying at some recent time.

When the silence became too much for me to bear, I said, "I'm sorry I doubted you."

He looked up at me, seeing me—really seeing me. He wet his bottom lip and said, "I'm sorry I gave you reason to doubt."

"Would you have really joined him?"

Samuel opened his mouth to speak and hesitated. He chewed over his words for a moment and shook his head. "Barker and I have a bond of blood."

"You're brothers?"

"We spilt blood together."

I nodded.

"That and…" He stared into his empty cup again. Out of some lingering sense of mercy I poured him another finger of whiskey.

121

When he'd taken a sip he continued. "We both of us got my sister's blood on our hands. I think we stuck together out of mutual guilt, but we nearly killed each other a dozen times over."

That struck me like a hammer to the chest. "I didn't know you had a sister."

"Kentucky was one of those places where they talk about 'Brother against Brother.'" He grunted. "I think she's why he always been such a zealot about the Yanks. Savannah and he…well, he and I had a principal disagreement about the secession. I didn't have a love for the Yankees, but it just felt wrong. Barker on the other hand…he talked her into runnin' away with him despite my best attempts to sway her otherwise. I went after 'em and caught the two of them down in Mississippi getting caught by a party of blue coats— General Halleck's boys—tromping through the woods.

"The fight was brief. Ugly."

He stared at the ceiling and I watched him. He did not look at me when he spoke next.

"I should'a been helping you, kid."

I tilted my head. "What?"

"You're suffering killer's remorse."

I felt my stomach sink. "Ah."

Samuel's hand reached out and gripped me by the shoulder. When I looked back up at him he was watching me with a closed, hurt expression. "It hit me real hard the first time I was forced to kill someone. I had to learn."

"Learn what?"

"This ain't a perfect world. Sometimes you have to kill."

I looked away, started to stammer excuses, but he caught me by the jaw and forced me to look at him. "Charlie—No, Charlie. Look at me.

"You listen hard. There's a balancing act going on you

122

can't afford to lose. You fall one way and you lose your heart—too scared to do what's right for fear of what it'll do to you. Fall to the other side and you lose your *soul*. You ever find yourself enjoying the sight of a man falling at your hands, it's time to hang up your irons because you've become a monster."

My chest hurt. I stared at him, and he stared back. I started to speak, but he interrupted me.

"Did you enjoy it?"

"No, Samuel. *God*, no."

"Good. And did it stop you from doing what's right?"

I hesitated, but he shook his head. "I understand you saved that girl. You defended yourself as well. No, Charlie, you're keeping your balance."

Samuel patted me on the cheek and rolled onto his back with a tired slump. He said nothing else for a long time. When the silence became intolerable I told him about the mirrors, the bodies, and about the coin's role. Samuel drank the words up, and I thought I could see him becoming harder, angrier as time went.

"And Daniel…" I hesitated at the look in his eyes, and finally fell quiet.

"Go on." The voice was like a knife sliding over a whetstone.

"Daniel agrees. He said the devil on the other side of that calling coin is giving them effective immortality. They can't be killed."

"Because they're already dead." His mouth twisted for a second and he spat. "Barker, you stupid goddamn snake."

Trouble on top of trouble. It seemed too much for Samuel. He rolled onto his side and took a stab at sleep. After everything, I let him have it.

123

The next day Doctor Thackery had Samuel moved back to the hotel. Bonehill and Daniel hemmed over the group's increasingly short funds and became nervous there would not be enough to pay for both the hotel and the doctor's services. They often sat together now, their heads bent close, deep in conversation about things they didn't need others to overhear. At first it was their devil-cursed brother in arms, but this new development added a second topic for these strained talks.

For the first week Samuel slept more often than not. I made sure he was fed, bringing meals up and cutting them into small portions so he would not have to strain. The doctor had prescribed good meat for his recovery, and laudanum for the pain. Samuel was happy for the former, but glowered whenever I tried to give him the latter.

"I ain't taking it," he'd say with a scowl.

"But the doctor…"

"Damn the doctor anyway. Pass me that bourbon."

Samuel spent his days asleep or working on going to sleep. When Daniel and Bonehill were not huddled together plotting Daniel was so thick in his own research that he might as well have been locked in another room. Bonehill surprised me. As much as he had groused about my presence he was spending every spare moment with Toby.

He didn't really know what to do with a girl grieving her family, but he did his best. I began to realize he felt an Atlas' weight of guilt for the death of her father and brothers. "It was my bullet what started the fire," he'd say to himself. Only once did he ask me for advice.

With all of this I was abandoned to my own devices.

That was where Maddy stepped in. At first she came to spend time with me in person. She'd bring a checkers board or books and we would read together—her small collection of occult books fascinated me, though I did not think back then to question as to why a lady of her quality would carry these things about.

Within a few days she was visiting with Samuel as well, taking over for his care to give me relief. Graham would take me, then, and we would go for a stroll or he would buy me lunch. I gathered he was a servant. Someone to look after Maddy Irving and keep her from getting into too much trouble. Though he seemed more inclined to follow along on her adventures, let her get into trouble, and make sure she wasn't killed along the way.

To my surprise he was a fine hand with a pistol. One morning I told him about the Dance revolver, about what Samuel had said about finding a balance.

"He's right, lad," Graham told me. "Miss Irving has told me something of the business you and your men are engaged in, and I think it is important that you possess strength to do what is right. But if you fall too much into the joy of it, you're liable to become a man like that Raleigh character."

Over the next few days of Samuel's recovery he took me shooting. It was a similar exercise to Samuel's: a fence and a line of bottles. Six bottles, with six cartridges. But now he timed me. The speed made me nervous. I rushed, and missed. But I got better, bit by bit.

Mister Graham and I were arriving back at the hotel one afternoon after one such excursion (and the inevitable trip back to the sheriff's office to return our guns) when I encountered Maddy leaving the room I shared with Samuel. Once more her hair was a tousled mess and her neckline unbuttoned. A lovely flush had risen on her cheeks.

"Tiresome woman!" Samuel shouted after her. "Close the damn door."

"Were you arguing again?" I asked her.

She laughed. "Yes, I guess we were."

"Samuel likes to argue."

She cupped my cheek, blessing me with another laugh. "He certainly makes a convincing point. His debate technique is *vigorous*."

Maddy sniffed, her face going dark. Something seemed to hang over her "Tiresome indeed."

God help me, I was a boy. It didn't help that I'd been brought up by a widower. I couldn't have seen what was right before me. And of course there was Samuel. Each time I found Maddy leaving like this I'd walk in on Samuel and find him a seething, smoldering wreck.

Still, the exercise must have been good for him. In a week's time they were taking brief walks together (Maddy mindful of his broken arm), though they always came back arguing. Within two weeks he was back at the table plotting with Daniel and Bonehill.

Maddy found Toby and I one morning sitting on the grand staircase of the hotel, watching them talk at a table in the far corner of the lobby. She sat beside me, knitting her fingers together restlessly as she watched them. We sat in silence for several minutes, and my train of thought turned from wondering what they were discussing to what she was thinking.

"It's their world," Maddy said with a blue note in her voice. She gave me a significant look. "I thought maybe 'twas just me but apparently they do not let anyone in."

"He talked to me more when they weren't around," I said, adding, "Not much, though."

"Mister Samuel Clayton keeps much to his chest."

"Tom is often quiet, often sad," Toby said. "But he talks to me. He told me about his hunting trips."

My brows rose in surprise. "Is that so?"

Toby nodded, curling her fist into the shape of a gun. She

pointed it at the hotel's chandelier. "I'm going to hunt down Barker Raleigh someday. I'll be a shootist just like Tom."

The silence regained its rule and the three of us sat together. Toby succumbed to boredom after a few minutes more watching and got up to find something else to do upstairs. When she was gone I spoke again.

"I learned something about him. He had a sister."

She frowned to herself. Maddy's face was made for frowns as much as it was made for smiles as I'm sure you well know—disapproving frowns, disappointed, lonely frowns. The two of you share that in common at the least. Today she gave a thoughtful frown.

"That explains that," she said, though more to herself.

"You're still working out Samuel's reading."

She pulled her shawl close, laughing without mirth. "That and three more I've performed since. The man is an enigma wrapped in wool and gun leather."

I thought about that first day at the card table—her playful banter buffeting like waves against the stone cliffs of Samuel's cold regard, the troubled look she'd given afterward, all the days before the gunfight at Toby's house when she had treated me with such warmth and him with such suspicion and confusion.

"The cards said something about the two of you," I said. "What was it?"

I expected her to tell me, as she had a thousand times, that a good reader does not betray the readings of another person. But she didn't. Instead she took a deep breath and let it out through her nose.

She leaned her shoulder against me, spoke as a close friend. "I'm not quite sure yet. Fondness, hatred—those two seem clear enough I suppose. We would stay together but be apart. Resent each other but cling fast. I don't know. Everything contradicts, and the picture changes each time I lay the cards out."

Maddy wet her lips. I looked behind her to find Graham at a polite distance, minding his own business. The man was omnipresent when it came to Maddy.

The men rose from their table, breaking up to go their own directions. Samuel turned towards us and stared at Maddy expectantly from across the room. She gave another of her pretty frowns.

"Time for the daily constitutional, I suppose. Charlie, won't you join us?"

I blinked. It hadn't occurred to me until now how natural their time alone had felt. I had to ask. "Why?"

"Because he may be less likely to argue if you're around."

"Then you don't know Samuel."

She chuckled without mirth. "I suppose I don't. Graham, I'm taking a stroll with Mister Clayton and Mister Kirchner. Would you see if October needs anything? Thank you, Graham."

Still, I joined them. The only acknowledgement Samuel gave was a flash of irritation when I joined them. Maddy held out her elbow and he took it with his good arm. The three of us walked into the warm sun to enjoy a little air and stretch our legs while we pondered the problem of Barker Raleigh.

Unfortunately, that was the day he decided to make an attempt on Samuel's life.

Chapter Sixteen

The Restless

"We're being followed," Samuel said, conversationally.

Maddy began to shift but he clutched her tight. "No. Don't move."

There was no shift in pace, nothing that might raise suspicion in those around us. I recognized what was happening only because Samuel had led me through this drill before. He led us on a round about course through Abilene, weaving through crowds of people (much to the vexation of disgruntled cowboys).

When twenty minutes of walking failed to throw our stalker Samuel muttered, "He's good."

We passed through a crowd of women ogling dresses in a storefront window and vanished into the alley between the dressmaker and a cobbler. The path Samuel chose wound behind and between the buildings that made up this commercial block of town. He practically dragged Maddy across the next major street and down six doors into another alley. I was left to jog behind them, flashing apologetic smiles at the rude stares we drew.

Samuel didn't rest until we stumbled upon a greasy belly taking a respite with his pipe behind a busy restaurant. The cook didn't seem too happy to share the back alley until he caught the look in Samuel's eyes. That was all it took to get the man indoors and back to work. Maddy stood beside Samuel, clutching her chest with a gloved hand and trying to regain her breath. I lagged behind.

"I think that should do it," he said.

I saw the figure rise from the other side of the restaurant

only a moment too late. I raised my hand and shouted, "Samuel!"

The shape resolved into a man I recognized from Raleigh's gang. Faster than I could track he shoved Maddy to the ground and pinned Samuel to the plank wall of the restaurant.

I reached for my Dance, but of course it wasn't there. Samuel, likewise unarmed, stared the man in the eyes. A sweat had broken out over Samuel's face as the bandit gripped him by his splinted arm. But he made no noise.

The man had a tobacco raspy voice. "Boss wants you, Clayton."

The bandit's other hand pressed something to Samuel's side. Shifting for a better view, I made out the form of a tiny gambler's gun.

Samuel's voice was cool, but the strain was obvious under the surface. "Not alive, I'd wager."

"Not until he knows where his trinket's got to. Personally, I'd as soon gut you and say you wouldn't give it up."

"Sounds treasonous," Samuel said. "You must not like what Raleigh's done to you."

The bandit squeezed Samuel's arm harder and I thought I heard a creak in my companion's voice. "You know nothing about it."

Raising his free hand defensively, Samuel said, "Whoa now. I'm not the one with his hat at a fightin' angle."

With another squeeze the Bandit said, "Where's the coin?"

Samuel grunted pain. Sweat dripped down his face now. "I know what you are."

"Shut your bone box, you son of a bitch! What ch'you know about it?"

"I know Raleigh's gone and sold the souls of all his fart-catchers."

I did not think it was possible for the man's face to get any

130

redder, yet it did. He pressed again and this time Samuel actually cried out in pain.

"Then you should know we cain't be killed! Where's the coin?"

"I also…" Samuel took a deep breath. "I also know something else."

"What's that?"

"I know you bastards still feel pain."

The bandit caught the glint in Samuel's eye and turned in time to see Maddy raise a hunting knife and bury it hilt deep in the man's eye. I stood by, far too stunned by the fight, by the brutal blow from Maddy, to say anything or react. Helpless, I watched the man scream and writhe, watched him flail and try to shoot Samuel with the little Derringer.

Samuel easily batted the hand away, and the gun fell to the dirt without a discharge. Try as he might, the bandit could not remove the knife. He clutched and clawed, and all his fingers drew was blood.

"Quick thinker," he said to Maddy as he grabbed her by the arm and hustled the two of us away from the scene.

We rushed out of the alley and down the next street, and after three blocks Maddy began to shake. I recognized this. I knew what was coming. Samuel distanced himself a little when she sank to her knees to sit on the stoop of a little one-room cabin, but I sat next to her and put my arm around her.

"First time?" I asked.

She nodded, staring at her hands. Her face was white, her lips pale and bloodless.

"Thought you knew how to acquit yourself," Samuel said. The look he gave her was not exactly disbelieving—not quite insulting.

The incredulity was enough to draw her out of it. She furrowed her brows and stared up at him. "I know how to shoot a rifle, Mister Clayton. I've chased off rustlers on cattle drives. It don't mean I ever had occasion to kill a man."

He spat in the dirt. "And you still haven't."

"Christ's blood," she said, taking a shaky breath. "That's right. It's a hard idea to reckon, stabbing a man through the eye and knowing he'll be fine."

"I think they're invulnerable," he said, "but they still need time to recover. It's why Raleigh was down after the shooting and the burial, why we had a few weeks before he sent someone after us."

The reminded me. "Do you still have the coin?"

"It's safe," was all he said on the subject.

"I can't believe you," Maddy said. "Charlie gives his life for you and you won't trust him with the coin. I *stabbed a man in the eye* and you question my steel?"

"No. What I did was distract you from your shakes. Too angry to be stunned now."

"You!" Her jaw flexed and worked. "You…!"

"Me." He smiled and turned to walk away. He stopped short at what he saw.

Wild Bill Hickok stood not ten yards off, leaning against a hitching post and cleaning his nails with a long knife. The sheriff whistled to himself until he noticed the three of us watching and tipped the flat brim of his cap to us. "Good afternoon ma'am, sirs. Interesting things a body overhears on his patrols."

The sheriff's office smelled like gun oil and fresh wood. Of the two cells only one was occupied; two cowboys sat within on their bunks playing a game of cards on a borrowed stool. The deputy jumped to his feet as soon as Hickok and the three of us entered.

"Athans," Hickok said to the man, "Mind doing a circuit of

the stock yards? Some of the bosses have been complaining about suspicious fellows loitering about."

The deputy nodded and tucked his piece into his coat pocket. When the deputy was gone Sheriff Hickok unlocked the cell and gave a jerk toward the door.

"Now that you boys are sobered up and friends again, git. Next time you want a drink, do so peaceably. I will not abide violence in my town unless it is committed at my hands."

When the room was cleared by for the four of us Hickok sat behind his desk. He gestured to Samuel's sling and asked, "How's the arm?"

"I can move it now." Samuel still bore a mustache of sweat from the bandit's grip, though twenty minutes had passed.

"You've made some interesting friends. Saw Ned Lingo— one of Raleigh's boys—following you three on your little constitutional. Thought I'd join in. Damndest thing, though. You vanished, then he vanished. Then you reappeared, and he didn't. There something I need to know? There been a killing in my town?"

Samuel stared back at him, stared through him. After a moment Hickok leaned back in his chair and kicked his feet up.

"No, I guess not. You'da come back here for the bounty if you had. So what happened to him?"

"We must have lost him," Maddy said, fluttering her eyes for the sheriff.

"Must have," Samuel agreed.

Hickok stared at the three of us awhile longer and leaned down to pull a bottle of good Union Star out of his desk drawer. "Care for a sip?"

"Don't mind if I do," Samuel said. Maddy joined him. My two heroes sat across a battered old desk over a bottle of whiskey. The two of them threw back their drinks.

"S'good," Samuel said.

"Only the best."

Maddy on the other hand knocked it back without so much as a flinch. When they glanced at her she raised a challenging brow.

Hickok cleared his throat and broke from her gaze. "Doc Thackery said your injuries were violence related."

"Related, yes," Samuel said.

The sheriff waited a moment for him to say more, but Samuel was Samuel. He waited for nothing, and when he realized it he shook his head and poured another round of whiskey all around.

"A man shows up in the middle of the night, shot, in a town with a prohibition against carrying firearms within city limits. This man belongs to a group of bounty hunters who have sworn they'd come to me as soon as they learned anything about the infamous Raleigh gang. I investigate a fire the next morning only to find three dead and signs that said gang had been occupying the premises.

"Does any of this sound familiar?"

Samuel could teach a rock silence.

"Then how 'bout this?" He resumed his tirade. "A boy mentions an injured man name Samuel—you *are* that Samuel, yes?—mere days after the violent abandonment of the Raleigh gang. This Samuel happens to be a part of aforementioned gang of bounty hunters. Are you still following me?

"Now here's where I personally became *rapt* with attention. The Raleigh gang has escalated even their prodigious amounts of violence in their robberies. More bodies, more gore. And everywhere they go they leave the message 'Bring me the coin, Samuel' written in the blood of their *God forsaken victims.* Does *that* ring any bells?"

By the end of it Hickok was gasping for breath, face red

with fury. He stared down the three of us. When I looked at Maddy I saw her face strained white. Samuel merely stared into the middle distance. When Samuel said nothing he leaned back in his chair and let out a slow breath.

"I'm working on a plan to catch them," Hickok said. He sipped his whiskey, swirling the drink around in his mouth, savoring it, before swallowing. "I got an idea but I'm going to need to assemble a good posse. You ever considered working *with* the law? I need someone who knows Barker Raleigh."

"What's the plan?" Samuel swirled the whiskey in his glass, staring at it.

"Need to lure him out. A trap. Since I can't seem to lay hands on this Samuel what's got him so riled up, I thought I'd make up a story 'bout money."

Maddy sat up at that. "False pretext? Wouldn't the trap work better if it were real money?"

"That would require me to be in possession of a ridiculous stack of coinage, miss…?"

With a manic grin she extended a gloved hand across the table to Hickok. He eyed the hand and the odd ring she wore. "Madeline Irving, daughter of *that* Irving. I'm needing to transfer some funds from the sale of our latest herd to my papa's bank in Chicago—about sixteen thousand dollars. Would that be suitable?"

The sheriff paled.

"You don't think it enough?" she said with a frown.

"Miss Irving," Hickok said, slapping the desk, "I think that would beat all!"

"Then you have my full cooperation."

"And you, sir? You'n yours would be sorely appreciated." Hickok turned back to Samuel, who was chewing his lip in thought.

"Hell, why not?"

Over the next few hours the three of them hashed out the details of the trap. It wasn't a bad idea—widely advertise the cargo in the right company, advertise the guard detail's political affiliation (and the name of one particular guard). Give the rumor a few days to ferment, spread, and they'd be ready. If any of Raleigh's boys were still in the area he would certainly hear about it. They knew at least one was already here.

Sunset was painting the sky a cedar pink when we returned to the hotel. I trailed behind Maddy and Samuel, keeping an eye on our rear, while the two strolled in their own little world. There was no further sign of Ned Lingo—it seemed the knife was enough of a deterrent.

The hotel's proprietor was lighting the lamps and chandelier when we walked in, and he nodded to the three of us. "Lovely day, marm. You're looking better, sir." We trailed up the stairs, Maddy giving Samuel extra support as he climbed. Bags clung beneath his eyes and despite the proprietor's pleasantries he looked sorely tired.

"He'll believe you have the coin," she said to Samuel as we crested the staircase, but she stopped. Graham awaited us, wringing his hands.

"I tried to stop them, m'lady. I tried to tell them, but Mister Bonehill bullied me out of the way."

"Tried to stop whom from what now?" Samuel asked. Their eyes turned down the balcony of the second floor and they saw the door to Maddy's room hanging open. Toby stood outside, her face twisted in a mixture of confusion and worry. Inside I could spy Bonehill turning the place upside down.

Maddy hiked up her skirt and marched down the balcony to the door, slamming it wide open. "What in blue hell is going on?"

Samuel and I weren't far behind her, rushing to keep up. The mattress had been pulled from its frame and all the drawers were opened, baring their contents all over the floor. What drew my eyes however were the collection of oddments around the room. A human skull carved in obscure sigils, a horn bound in iron and jewels, jewelry as curious as what Maddy already wore.

Daniel stood to one corner, blushing to be caught going through her things. Naturally he'd found a small stack of rare books in her possession and had been reading through them. Bonehill bore none of his shame. He sniffed and looked her up and down.

"What's the meaning of this?" Maddy said, her face flushing.

Bonehill set a bust of a falcon head he'd been looking at on the bed. "I'd ask you the same thing, lady." From his pocket he drew a velvet bag. Turning it out a coin dropped in his hand, old and worn, bearing a familiar inscription.

"You stole the calling coin?" Samuel turned on her and she threw her hands up.

"Stole, Samuel? I just wanted to look at it, that's all."

Daniel snapped the book shut, shaking his head. "Obscure occult texts and grimoires, a collection of curious spirit fetishes and cursed items, statues of long dead gods. Did you steal all of these, Maddy?"

Her eyes darted around the room, taking in all of us. I suspect she didn't realize she started to take small shuffling steps back toward the corner. "I can't believe you think I stole it."

"I found it laying on your dresser like it weren't nobody's but yours." Bonehill held the coin up between his thumb and trigger finger.

"I'd have—I'd have paid you for it. I still will, when this is all over. Surely you don't need it anymore."

"I suspect we will," Daniel said. "It's the crux of the Raleigh conundrum. A body has to wonder what you were doing with it in your possession."

She drew herself upright, fingers tightly clutching the skirt of her dress where it met her waist. A deep breath and her voice came out schooled, cold. "I am a collector of supernatural curiosities, gentlemen. I promise you each of these I have paid for with proper money. Some were auctions, some I bought off private collectors, or in estate dealings."

"Why?" Samuel took a step toward her. His voice was deadly still. "That coin is trouble. Half these things in here are trouble."

"Why is my own business. I'm a collector and that's all you need to know—and do not give me that condescending look. I'm not the only one holding a secret here. You four are just as guilty. Your stake in this isn't because you know Raleigh. Your stake in this is because you hunt creatures."

She gave a derisive sniff. "Bounty hunters indeed."

"Is that why you've clung to us?" Bonehill asked. "Samuel, ain't I told you not to let this lady come sniffing around? If a nag comes nosing at your hand she wants food, not company."

Samuel's cold regard was turned on Bonehill next and he quieted down. When Bonehill was seen to, Samuel turned back to Maddy and began to stalk toward her. For each step he took forward she took one back until she was well and truly backed into the corner A hand rested on the hilt of his knife as if she might spring at him at any moment.

"You're going to return the coin to us and you're going to leave town." His words were the deadly whisper of a snake over leaves. His eyes were as Medusa's, freezing her where she stood. "And you will never see us again."

She could not let him tarnish her dignity however. Maddy

worked up her courage and drew herself straight again. "I saw it in the cards, Samuel. You need me, and you're willing to pay me handsomely for it."

"I'm willing to let you leave this town with your life."

The collective tension of the room rose sharply. There was a general shuffling—a gasp from Toby. Out of the corner of my eye I saw Graham reaching into his coat for some hidden weapon.

"You wouldn't hurt a woman," Maddy said with a quaver in her voice.

There was nothing but conviction in Samuel's. "Try me."

"The coin is in one of my books," she said hastily tearing her eyes away from him. "A Goetic appendix. The one with the mauve cover."

She remained pressed against the wall, licking her lips. Her eyes darted over to Daniel while he hastily whipped through the appendix. His eyes went wide when he found the page.

"She wasn't bluffing, Samuel. Look." He held the book forward for us to see. I saw the seal inscribed on the coin, notations about the inscription and the creature it summoned.

"Raleigh's summoned a real bastard, Samuel," Daniel said. "This Wither. He's a Duke of the Crossroads."

"What is it?" Maddy asked. "I saw the phrase but I didn't understand it."

Daniel cleared his throat, and I sensed one of his lectures coming on. "The Crossroads Dukes, they're akin to hell's stumpers, politicians, and merchants in one. They recruit by offering something you want more than anything. Tit for tat, but tat tends to be the damnation of your eternal soul."

"Haven't heard of Wither," Samuel said. "What's his real name?"

Daniel took the book back and began to read, his finger tracing lines. "Here, his proper name is Lashonael. It means…thinking…yes, it means 'Tongue of God.'"

The hairs on the back of my neck stood on end, and behind me I heard a moan of despair from Toby. "My da's murderer trucks with demons? This can't be real."

To my surprise Bonehill laid a hand on her shoulder. "We're used to dealing with this, kid. It's alright to be scared. Don't worry, we'll see him and all his restless boys six feet under."

Daniel chortled. "'The Restless.' That's a good name for this unliving phenomenon." He pulled his Bible from his pocket and made a notation.

"Scared nothing." She looked up at him with hard eyes. "What can I do to help?"

"Don't think that's a good idea," Samuel said.

Bonehill's eyes narrowed. "If we're holding kids back then we best be leaving him behind, too."

"Charlie's in this business already, and he can handle himself."

"So can I!" Toby pulled from Bonehill and marched to Samuel. "I can handle myself, Mister Clayton. I know how to shoot, and I can fight. Please—he killed my family. Let me help."

Muttering something about bad precedents, Samuel tore his eyes from her. That was when Maddy decided to throw her hat in the ring.

"I'm helping too."

"The hell you are," Samuel growled. "You've got a train to catch."

"You're right—a train with my company's profits. Or did you think Raleigh and his boys would show up if you asked nicely? You need bait, and as I see it you need bait that folk won't think of as fishy. Or would you rather just print 'Monster Hunter with Demon Coin Riding East on Train at

Dawn!' all over the broadsheets?"

His response was a growl. When neither of the other two hunters spoke up I tugged at his sleeve saying, "She's right Samuel. We need her help."

"Bad business. Don't want two women along, much less a lady and a girl."

Maddy rolled her head back and groaned. "God save us from chivalry. I already promised my help to Sheriff Hickok. Graham and I are already pledged to the cause. Think of it as a service provided in exchange."

"In exchange for what?"

"I want a fair share of Raleigh's gold. And the coin."

Bonehill took a step forward. "Now see here, missy. You got more money'n God. What do you need that for?"

"My *Father* has the money. Do you know why he exiled me to your nation Mister Bonehill?" She gestured at her arcane collection. "He didn't approve of me using his funds to further my interests. He hoped to whip me into shape. I aim to have some capital of my own to resume my collections."

"No deal," Samuel said. "The money belongs to Raleigh's victims."

"But," Maddy said.

"No!" Bonehill said.

"But Charlotte," Daniel protested.

Samuel stabbed with his finger to underscore each word. "The money. Don't. Belong. To. Us. She can have the coin—"

Daniel protested louder. "Samuel, no!"

"*After* we make use of it. And not a second sooner."

"Picked a hell of a time to grow a conscience, Clayton," Bonehill muttered, turning away. That earned a dirty look from Samuel, but he said nothing.

"We don't need her help, Samuel," Daniel said, crossing the room to stand between him and Maddy. "We can think of

141

something else."

I knew what Samuel was thinking when he avoided Daniel's eyes, when he stared at the floorboards. "We don't have the luxury of time, Daniel. Hickok told us Raleigh's carving folk up, using their blood to paint taunts directed at me. The sooner we do this, the fewer people have to die."

Daniel huffed, but did not argue the point. He shook his head, his voice going quiet. "Fine. I can see in your eyes that you have a plan. What's the first step?"

"The first step is we have a sit down with this Wither."

Chapter Seventeen

The Tongue of God

Preparations were made according the book, the book being our Charlotte Bibles. The Dukes are creatures of transition and choice. Toby gave us our site of calling—a crossroads near the ruins of her home. Maddy's book gave us the time of calling—during the golden hour or as the book put it "When day and night combine." Daniel's research noted down in our Bibles gave us our precautions.

A circle was drawn seven feet across in the ashes of a cedar tree laced with salt. We lit seven candles to close the prison and placed them around the circle. Samuel's personal experience gave us the last precaution—the candles were placed in sturdy glass lanterns to guard them against blowing out.

At his insistence Maddy and Toby were made to stay in town.

When everything was in place we began the calling. Bonehill built a hot fire within the trap circle, careful not to disturb the ashes when he entered or exited. Valuables would need to be burned within the fire—precious to entice our mark.

With a pained look Daniel gave up a slim manuscript bound in pale leather. "Such knowledge lost to mankind."

"For the greater good, Daniel," Bonehill said.

Bonehill sacrificed one of his last Whitmore bullets (removing the powder first to make sure we didn't kill ourselves). Samuel offered up a lock of hair bound in ribbon which I had never seen before. I shot a questioning look at Bonehill but he shook his head—better not to ask. It took some coaxing from the two of them to goad me into giving up my sacrifice, but at last I did it. I pulled my signed copy of *On a Springfield Evening* from my coat pocket and laid it in Samuel's waiting hand.

He threw the sacrifices onto the fire. The hair and the paper caught immediately, the casing and bullet began to twist and deform. Bonehill tossed the coin into the fire, where it gleamed and reflected more of the light than something so old and tarnished should have. Joining hands, the three of us stood before the flames and the candles and we intoned, "We call you, Wither."

We listened, our ears straining for the coming of the demon. I didn't know what to expect, but I didn't think it was this. The wind hardly stirred over the plains, and mid summer birds hooted and called. Overhead the first bats of the night were taking wing. But there was nothing else.

"Try it again," Samuel said. His eyes stared into the fire, sharp as flint.

"We call you, Wither."

We called again, and again, and again. But there was no response from the Duke of the Crossroads. Breaking away from us Samuel rounded on Daniel.

"Are you sure that's the ceremony?"

Throwing his hands up, Daniel stuttered, "Th-that's what the book said!"

We watched as Samuel turned away and pulled his hat off to scrub at his hair. "Damn shyster demon can't even come when called."

A voice, reedy and thin, spoke from behind us, at the fire. "The shyster demon prefers to get a measure of his prospective clientele first."

My heart leapt into my mouth and I spun to face the fire. Around me I heard the scrape of guns being drawn from leather. A figure floated in the fire, roughly the shape of a man, but badly proportioned.

"Lashonael," Daniel said.

"In the flesh." The Tongue of God, Duke of the Crossroads swept a fine beaver fur top hat from a head with a Texas steer's long horns and a face like a desiccated corpse. He gave us a lipless smile as he took a bow. As he did, he spoke with a refined tongue.

"Gentlemen, you may call me Wither. This humble servant asks how he may assist three such accomplished hunters." There were no eyes in those sockets, only two blue pinprick fires, yet somehow I could read that he was taking us in, that those eyes were smiling at a joke only he could hear.

As he bowed I realized I could not see feet. The fire burned unnaturally tall and hot, blue at the tips. And it was there that the form of the demon merchant of crossroads formed his body—out of the flames, just above the knees. From this perspective he looked down over us, seeming ten feet tall.

"What shall it be, messieurs?" As he spoke he turned to look at each of us in turn. "Lost knowledge long forgotten, Mister Garner? A lifetime's fill of wine, women, and song, Mister Bonehill (and my good man, may I say, I *adore* your surname)? A reunion with your lost family, Young Mister Kirchner?"

A shiver danced up my spine when he looked at me. But a moment later he turned his gaze upon Samuel. His voice became quiet, thoughtful, as he considered my mentor.

"Or something more special perhaps? How would you like a taste of the coming retribution?"

"We're here about a customer of yours," Samuel said, meeting the demon in the eyes.

Wither ran skeletal hands with bulbous bony knuckles over the material of his exquisitely tailored suit. "The coming retribution, then. I think you will find my prices quite reasonable. All I ask—"

"Is our souls," Bonehill said.

"Boilerplate contract," Daniel added.

Samuel shook his head. "Not ours to give, demon."

Wither gave a chuckle like the sound of bones rattling in a coffin. "The gentlemen have been reading too much Goethe. I *said* my prices are reasonable. Speak your request."

"Information on Barker Raleigh," Samuel said. "What you did to him, how to stop him."

"And what are you willing to give me in return?"

The hunters all looked at each other.

Wither tapped his jagged chin with one of those claw-like fingers. "You know, it has been *such* a long time since I've eaten a good rack of ribs. There is a girl in your company…"

Bonehill growled and reached for his gun again.

The demon threw up his hands, laughing. "Joking! Joking…humans lack sufficient meat for my tastes. I will do you a favor, and in exchange you will do a favor for me."

Samuel asked, "What's the favor?"

"I want you to collect Barker Raleigh's soul."

That drew confused looks from the present company. Daniel scratched his head and asked, "I thought he was working with you? Why do you want us to kill him?"

"My reasons are my own, but to be succinct he has failed in fulfilling his end of our contract."

Samuel crossed his arms, eyes narrowing. "And if we fail?"

"*Then* I get your souls." Wither cackled, tapping his fingertips together.

Again the three hunters looked at each other. Agreement passed silently between them and as one they looked at me.

"You're a part of this too, Charlie," Daniel said.

"If'n you want to back out, now's the time," Bonehill

added.

I looked at them, and back up to the towering form of the Duke. Samuel took me gently by the back of the neck and turned my head to look at him. His stern face frowned down at me, lit in eerie shadows by the demon's blue fire.

"You can walk away if you want, Charlie. This is our fight. You got no stake in it."

The truth was, my stomach clenched so hard from fear that I thought I might throw up. My lip trembled, my palms were slick with sweat, and so was my spine. I could walk away now.

I shook my head. "You're my friends. This is my fight, too."

"Brave boy," Wither purred. "Now, our arrangement."

"You have our word," Samuel said. "Raleigh's dead."

"Not yet, but soon I trust. Very well. Our bargain is struck."

The evening air flashed with unseen energy and I felt as though I'd been swiftly grabbed by the back of my neck and squeezed. My vision sparkled and my breath came short. And as soon as it came over me, it was gone.

Around me, puzzled faces and clenched hearts told me I was not the only one struck with the unseen hand. A vein throbbed on Samuel's face and I thought he would turn on Wither then and there. But he took a deep breath to steady himself.

"Alright, you got your claws in us. Tell us what we need to know."

"In a town between lands, haunted by the past—"

Samuel drew the Remington. He stared Wither down the spine of the gun, his face cold. "I have exactly no time for riddles, peddler. Tell us straight or our bargain is annulled."

"Idle threats," Wither scoffed.

"I'm packing silver in my rounds, and the tips have been

stamped with Solomon's seal."

"It won't kill me."

"It'll sting like black Hell."

Wither's throat caught. But he complied.

"Barker Raleigh is gathering an army."

Daniel cleared his throat. "We know. He intends to restore the Confederacy."

"He has no such desires." The Demon cracked a smile—soured by the sight of the Remington still trained on him. "He recruits men at a fevered pace—his gang is now larger than any other bandit gang in this territory. He arms them and transfers his own gift unto them for one purpose: to raze the District of Columbia to the ground."

Bonehill muttered a curse to himself and Daniel shook his head. But there was no sign of disbelief on Samuel's face.

"What was the gift?" he asked.

"Effective immortality. Though his body be defiled, his spirit remains."

"Also defiled," Bonehill said.

Wither tapped the rim of the hole where his nose should have been. "Just so. And please bear in mind that he may grant his gift to others in his company should they agree to drink a portion of his blood. But they must *agree*."

"So how do we weigh anchor on his spirit?" Samuel asked.

"On the Missouri-Kansas border you will find the cadaver of a town once known as Jericho. There is a graveyard in that town, and in that graveyard a tree. On this tree, in this graveyard, in this town, there hang six men—followers who gave their lives unwillingly. These are his anchors. Cut them down and he will be free to fly from his walking corpse."

"And this will affect the others, too?" Daniel asked.

"Barker Raleigh is the pin upon which the whole mechanism rests."

148

The hunters shared a look and nodded.

Nearby, Bonehill crouched at the circle and stared at the coin in the burning center. "Interesting, this calling coin. I assume one needs the coin to keep calling you up."

The demon tapped his fingertips together, his face a rictus grin.

"So how did he forget the coin?" Bonehill asked.

"As I've mentioned, I am disappointed with our mutual acquaintance's erratic fulfillment of our bargain. It was time to find someone to help…terminate his contract."

That hung in the air over us. All along, manipulated by an unseen demon into doing his bidding.

Wither cleared his throat. "A final note. Raleigh and his men have gotten creative with their gift. Some have learned to stitch animal parts to their own anatomy in place of existing limbs—you may find them challenging. Now then, our business is concluded," Wither said. With another doff of his hat he vanished into the fire. As the fire died the demon's voice spoke into the night air offering one last admonition. "Enjoy cutting those bodies down. They have a kind of immortality too. They'll be quite…ripe."

Without the demon the fire guttered down to a coal's glow and soon died. All that was left was the last rays of the day and the candlelight.

"A hanged-man tree," Daniel said wonderingly. "I'd heard about such a thing, but the details of what it would confer on its creator were foggy at best."

"No time to ponder now, Danny." Samuel flexed his bad hand, staring down at it. "Posse lays the trap tomorrow. We need to make plans."

"Animal parts? Suppose he meant the man with the arm?" Bonehill stroked his sharp beard, staring up at the evening's first stars. "Were I Raleigh, I'd want to keep an eye on that

149

tree."

Samuel agreed. "I'd wager good money on the treasure being in Jericho. Sounds like we have what we need. Let's get home, boys."

Chapter Eighteen

The Rolling Trap

Samuel shook me awake before dawn. My senses returned from sleep and I looked around, my head filled with cotton. I was sitting in the chair, and with dread I realized I'd fallen asleep on the watch.

"If you were getting sleepy, you should'a woke me."

"You're injured, and today's a big day…" I couldn't meet his eyes.

"Injury wouldn't matter if one of his boys busted in here and killed us both while we slept."

"Samuel—I'm sorry."

He smiled when I apologized, and that was what told me something was wrong.

Without even the light of a lantern we dressed in the cold hotel room. I splashed water on my face and scrubbed sleep from my eyes while he pulled his jacket on over his bad arm.

We were almost out the door before I realized he wasn't wearing his sling. "Samuel, your arm isn't fully knitted."

"I'm still wearing the splint, boy. You're as bad as Doc Thackery."

"Samuel…"

"It'll only get in the way. Go on, we're on a schedule."

Bonehill and Daniel met us on the balcony and the four of us walked down together, silent as stones. Only a lamp on the desk, and the faint light at the windows lighted the lobby. We crept across the floorboards, conscious of making any noise.

A shape formed out of the black between two windows and my heart nearly stopped. Before I could die of shock, however, the shape resolved into the form of Toby.

It wasn't until that moment, in her quiet burning anger, that I realized that she was actually several inches taller than me. I realized it was more likely we were of age, and it was obvious she outclassed me in size.

"You said you'd take me," she said with a voice like cracking frost.

"Toby..." Bonehill said.

"No! You said you'd take me."

Samuel gave me a glance so quick I almost didn't notice it. He sized her up and nodded. "Fall in, soldier."

Beyond the hotel the morning air was unseasonably cool and the world was damp with dew. We made it almost to the sheriff's office before our next interruption. At the intersection of two streets we found Madeline Irving waiting for us, Graham in her shadow.

"And just where the hell do you think you're going..."

It was Samuel's turn to falter, but he failed at that. His face could have been carved from ice for how he looked at her.

"I suppose you thought to ride off with my money and go back on your bargain, is that it?" she asked, stepping forward. "Glad I put a stop to that. Now, let's go."

"Not your money," he said.

"T'aint yours either. Enough dawdling—let's go. Graham?"

The butler followed her as she turned briskly toward Hickok's office. The menfolk shared a dubious look, though I laughed to myself when Samuel wasn't looking. Jaw outthrust, Toby marched after Maddy like a soldier.

A crowd of perhaps fifteen hard-looking men waited for us outside the sheriff's office. It was an eclectic crowd—honest-looking farmers, rough and tumble cowboys, a pair of gentlemen in fine black suits, and I even recognized a few storeowners. When Hickok spied us coming his way he nodded and addressed the crowd. "Seems the last of our party

152

has decided to join us. Step up, gentlemen."

Hickok explained the plan to the crowd, though we six were acquainted with it. He introduced Maddy and explained that Miss Irving's company would be transporting profits from the latest cattle drive East for safe keeping in Chicago. Rumor had been allowed to circulate that she was moving upwards of sixteen thousand dollars and that she was looking for good, honest, Union men. He did not mention that rumor of the identity of some of the guard had been allowed to circulate.

What he did not know—could not be allowed to know—was that the gold and the robbery were now to serve as a distraction. Tom Bonehill, Toby McMillen, Maddy Irving, and myself were to get off the train at a small country station on the border and make way for Jericho. Hopefully to counteract Raleigh's advantage in war.

The previous night we had drawn straws to determine who would be the ones to go. It was dubious circumstances that the woman and both children ended up drawing the short straws, though Samuel never admitted to rigging the drawing.

Weapons were passed out and we all claimed ours with visible notes of relief on the faces of the veterans in our company. When my gun belt—rolled around the holster and the Dance—came out of the barrel I walked up to claim it and got shoved out of the way by a blond man with hair curling out of the open chest of his shirt.

"Out of the way, boy. Don't lay hands on a man's weapon."

"That's my gun!" I protested, drawing looks ranging from amusement to pure surprise.

"Obviously lying," he said to the others holding it out. "Who'd give a kid a full rig?"

The question seemed obvious to the rest of the crowd. Not everyone carried their irons in a holster. Most were content to tuck in pockets or into their belts.

The sound of a match striking, of a cigarillo catching fire, could not be heard of the chuckles of the men gathered.

"If you knew his skill with a pistol you'd know he earned that gun." Samuel's voice cut through the crowd like chill iron.

Men fell silent and all turned to look at him. I saw Hickok's eyes narrow and a hand drift toward the pistol slung across his belly.

"Give it back. That weapon's not yours," Samuel said.

"Says who?"

"Says the piss-poor state of your clothes. No man who takes that poor a care of himself would keep a gun in such fine condition."

Despite my nervousness, I felt my heart thud with pride.

"And you know it's his because…?"

"Because I gave it to him." He looked all around. "To celebrate his first bounty kill."

That set the men to talking again. Each appraised me in a new light. The burly man, seeing support from the crowd vanishing, began to stammer. It took a word from Hickok to finish what Samuel started.

"The gun belongs to the boy. Hand it back to him now like an adult. Yeah, that's good. Hate to have to take you in for theft."

I took my guns (earning another round of gossip when I took the Sharps) stepped off the boardwalk and moved to rejoin the other hunters, strapping the gun on over my suspenders. The solid weight at my hip sent tremors of relief mixed with dismay. It was a tool for killing, after all. Nothing would change that. But I remembered a certain Charlotte brother saving a little German boy's life at gunpoint. I could do the same.

"Let's get this trap a-rollin'!" Hickok shouted, and the men fell in.

The lockbox with the money was taken from the sheriff's office, carried by two men under Graham's supervision. The butler's hands held his coat back to reveal one hand resting on the rosy red grip of a pistol, daring someone to come after the money.

The posse surrounded that lock box and walked it to the train station where our ride awaited, chuffing steam into the morning air. It was the strangest funeral procession I've ever borne witness to. Once aboard we spread out amongst the waiting train cars. Samuel and Daniel were left with Hickok and two other men in the car with the lockbox, and we waited in the car just ahead of them. Maddy shared a bench with me, Graham sitting across from us with a placid expression; across the aisle Toby sat with Bonehill.

Toby gave me a second's nervous smile, and bit her lip. Her skin was pallid, and I thought she might be sweating. "Back where we started—ay, Springfield Charlie?"

"What? No, it's a Sharps."

"No—it's—do you remember when we met? On the train, you couldn't talk."

That day months ago came rushing back. At the remembrance I half laughed. "Right."

"Samuel's not your Da, though." Her smile faltered, and I knew what she was thinking.

"You don't stop missing them," I said. "But it hurts. My Papa's been gone a year now. Sometimes I still wake up crying. The sound of bullfrogs gives me nightmares. But the pain dulls a little."

"Thanks," was all she said, turning to look away from me.

To the side of me I realized Maddy was studying me. She was quiet, and her gaze felt like a stone on my shoulders. I tried to smile for her and to her credit she tried to smile back.

The train's whistle blew, drawing startled shouts from Toby and I both. Only one other man from the posse sat in our car—one of the dapper-dressed men—and he laughed. Toby gave him a sour glare, but I knew the laugh was good-natured. A moment after the whistle the train shuddered to life, and the world outside the windows began to crawl past us.

Each man or woman in our party bided their time in their own way. Bonehill checked and rechecked his kit, going over his six guns and the Whitworth each a dozen times. Toby hummed to herself a tune I came to realize was the same song Maddy had sung to me two and a half weeks before. Maddy and I occupied ourselves with her cards. She carried the Tarot deck with her today, and she walked me through each of the cards, introducing me to the major and minor arcana. Naturally, when she offered to let me draw a card I drew the Fool once more.

Though the train bore no passengers but the engineer and the posse, the train made regular stops at stations along the line to keep the outward appearance of normal operation. When Bonehill wasn't scrubbing his guns he was checking a battered pocket watch he kept in that deerskin jacket of his.

"Nervous?" the dapper-dressed man asked him.

Bonehill said nothing.

Moments later our bodies lurched with the motion of the train slowing. Toby and I stood at once, wobbling on our legs but the dapper man checked his own watch and gave us a placid look.

"Just a little jerkwater town. We've been running long enough to need water."

"I gotta take a piss," Bonehill announced to the cabin. Casually he stood up and walked to the forward door of the car, waving a hand to us. "Stretch your legs, boys and girls."

If I had not known the lie I would never have suspected. The water stop was our agreed upon breakaway point since that would be so near to the border. We were reaching the end of the Kansas Pacific territory. Smoothing my face I followed after Bonehill and soon heard the footsteps of Maddy and Toby falling in behind me. At the crinkling of a newspaper I looked over my shoulder and saw the dapper-dressed man watching us closely, but he did not rise from his seat.

"That man's up to something," I said once the door to the car was shut behind us and I was climbing off the train.

"Aye, my skin prickles when I feel him looking at us," Maddy said.

The town was insignificant, hardly a handful of buildings surrounding the water tower. The station was nothing more than a platform. Still, it bustled with men moving to and fro. Two men worked the water chute where only one should have been necessary, and I saw another two or three talking to the engineer. A couple of fellows, lost, seemed to be trying to get on.

I opened my mouth to say something when Bonehill jerked and darted back into the shadow between train cars. He grabbed Maddy and Toby each and dragged them back with us. Maddy began to protest but he clamped a hand over her mouth. A moment later Graham snatched me back into the shadow with them.

"You saw them, too?" Bonehill asked the butler.

Graham nodded.

"What?" Maddy asked.

The butler's face was grim. "Miss Irving, I recognized Raleigh's men amongst the townsfolk here."

That was the moment gunfire broke out.

Most of the pops were coming from the head of the train, the engine. When I peeked around the corner I could see the

157

white haze of spent powder rising into the air. The sight of it formed a lead ball in my stomach.

"We leave now," Bonehill said.

I spun on him. "But Samuel!"

"Will be six feet under if we don't undo Wither's gift."

I bit my lip, staring at the black iron grating between our feet. I knew he was right, but the thought of abandoning Samuel, and abandoning Daniel to this, left a sour twist in my gut.

"We'll need horses," Maddy said.

"We can steal 'em." Bonehill leaned out of our little hiding spot. We waited the span of several heartbeats for him to say anything, and at last he nodded. He shouldered his Whitworth case and darted out onto the platform, jumped off the far end, and ducked into the shadow of a house. Behind him Graham's face soured at the prospect of theft.

One by one we followed. First Toby, then Maddy, then I ran out into the open. The sound of gunfire still peppered the air as I exposed myself, joined by the screams of the dying and orders barked out by Hickok and his deputies. I feared at any moment Barker Raleigh himself would step out from the train and level his pistol on me.

Building by building we made our way across the little jerkwater town until we found four horses tethered at the same stand. It was a straight shot—all we had to do was cross a yard, jump a fence, and they were ours. So naturally a cluster of Raleigh's men stood nearby.

"They still hurt," Maddy muttered beside me, as if reading our thoughts.

Bonehill nodded, drawing back the hammer of his six-gun. He glanced back in my direction as he spoke. "If we can surprise them we may be able to get the horses and light out. You gonna be alright with this, kid?"

"I'll do what I have to do." I drew my Dance and checked the cylinder.

"On the count of three, then:

"One."

"Two."

"Three."

He opened up, catching a man in the chest. A second man was pegged across the side of his head. Our resident marksman was making each bullet count. They returned fire, but soon we joined our violence with Tom Bonehill's and created a withering storm that sent them to cover, cussing.

"Now!" Graham shouted.

We sprinted across the yard and leapt the fence. All the while Maddy kept up a storm of lead with her rifle. Bonehill jumped into the stirrups of one horse and lifted Toby into the saddle with him. As I approached mine a bullet bounced off the hitching post, and the horse I was reaching for pulled out of his tether and bolted.

"No time!" Maddy called to me. She grabbed me by the arm and hauled me bodily into the saddle with her.

"Go! Go!" Bonehill whipped his reins and we were off.

Chapter Nineteen

Dead Jericho

I can tell you now that I dreaded the passing of each minute that we spent on horseback. The sound of gunfire haunted us, chased us, across the wide Kansas plain. We rode hard, knowing there was only ten miles to the river dividing Kansas and Missouri. Only ten miles to Jericho.

I was uncomfortable, sitting in Maddy's lap, doing nothing but waiting. So it was that I often checked the surrounding landscape. It was only by that grace that I saw the cloud of dust coming up behind us.

"We're being chased!"

I just made out the sound of Bonehill's cursing over the pounding of our hooves. He passed his revolver to Toby and she began to slide fresh cartridges in.

Maddy thrust the reins in my hand with barely a "Hold this." No sooner did I have control than she was slotting cartridges into her rifle. I guided the horse while she turned and sighted down the Henry's barrel.

Graham fired the first shot. The butler moved with a soldier's professionalism, reins gripped firmly in his teeth.

"Faster!" Bonehill shouted. "We can't let them catch up with us."

I sawed at the reins, dug my heels into the horse's sides. I felt Maddy shift behind me and a moment later my ears rang with the crack of the rifle. When my hearing cleared I could make out the distant thunder of Raleigh's men returning in kind.

Those last miles were tense. Their shadows drew nearer, and several times I felt the wind of flying lead rush past my

160

body. We rode so fast and so hard my body began to ache with the effort of it. When I thought I might lose myself I saw the town spring into sight.

We crested the top of a river-sculpted hill. There it was, below us, on the banks. Perhaps ten or so buildings remained standing, many more reduced to black timber. Jericho spread out in the crook of two hills along the river, plants already beginning to reclaim the place that man had abandoned.

The remains of a road materialized halfway down the slope into town and we rode quickly in and among the rotting structures. A hill standing between us and Raleigh's boys all we could hear was the caw of crows picking over the Jericho's bones.

Bonehill searched the place, always moving, always wary. "Been empty maybe two years, three. Fire tore through the place. Quantrill's doing, maybe?"

"Or Raleigh's," Maddy said.

I shuddered.

"Cemetery's up the next rise," Bonehill said. "I think I see the tree."

It was hard not to. The cemetery stood above the town, beside a clapboard church sore in need of whitewash. In the center stood a skeletal tree, ash or oak perhaps, leafless. It may have been my eyes playing tricks, but I thought I could see its six grisly apples dangling by their stems.

"They're still coming," Maddy said from behind me. I strained and thought I could hear the pounding of hooves. "Charlie, I'm getting off here. Graham and I will thin the herd."

"Maddy, that's—"

"T'isn't suicide, young one." She swung off the saddle in a flash of white petticoat. Upon landing she laid a hand on my chest and smiled. "Not so long as you get them bodies down

161

right quick."

"Time's wasting," Bonehill said, heeling his horse back into motion.

She turned and rushed away, her bustle bobbing behind her. Graham gave us a tip of the hat and muttered "Good luck."

I watched the forms of Maddy and her servant vanish into a two-story house. When they'd disappeared into the black within I too rode up the hill.

There is a word to express the feeling you have riding through towns like Jericho: Kenopsia. I heard Daniel use it once and had to ask him what he'd said. It is the peculiar forlorn prickling of your emotions at seeing a place you realize should be alive with people but is now empty and dead. Jericho radiated kenopsia, and the feeling only intensified as we drew nearer to the cemetery.

Indeed the land seemed to feel it as well. Trees grew barren. Grass grew yellow. Even the crows kept their distance. When I could first make out the shapes of the hanged men, in truth rather than imagination, the hair on the back of my neck stood on end. There it was, the birth of Barker Raleigh's dread gift.

"O Death, where is your sting?" I recited to myself. That earned a glance from Bonehill. Toby was too distracted by the sight of the dead men to say anything. A sickly green was rising in her pallor.

"Goodness God, kid!" Bonehill barked. "Get off the horse if you're gonna chuck!"

He hurried off the side of the horse, dragging her off a moment later. As soon as her boots hit the dirt she keeled over and retched onto the thirsty earth. The splash narrowly missed Bonehill's boots.

He slid away from her, giving her the privacy to finish upending breakfast, and began to unpack his Whitworth.

"Only a few of these left," he said to the two of us. "We'll need to make them count. Charlie, since I know how you shoot I want you down here with me. Lead starts to fly as soon as we can make 'em hurt."

He jerked a single edged hunting knife from his belt and offered it hilt-first to Toby who was just wiping off her mouth on her sleeve. "I want you up in the tree cutting down bodies."

"Tom, no…" she said. "I get queasy just lookin' at 'em."

He clenched his eyes shut for a moment, taking a deep breath. Before Bonehill could be Bonehill I broke in and spoke on Toby's behalf.

"She knows her way around a rifle and she can do that without having to look at the bodies. I can get up the tree and start chopping them down."

"Fine. Do it." He passed the knife to me instead.

Below us in the town we heard the opening volleys of Maddy's trap. The sound came up to us, bounced several times over off the surrounding hills.

"Today, Charlie! Today!"

"Right. Today." I took a deep breath to steady my nerves and clenched the knife between my teeth.

The tree stood over me like a claw reaching up to heaven to curse it. I tried not to let the distant pop of bullets rattle me while I grabbed the trunk and dug my toe into a small crook.

My hands found purchase on knobs, small branches. I pulled myself up by a toe here and a hand there. A branch began to protest under my foot and I had to throw myself at the next limb up.

My hands slipped on the smooth bark of the tree and I clawed for purchase. With a mighty grunt of desperation I kicked away from the trunk and heaved my legs up to grip the branch.

When I at last was able to pull myself upright on the

163

branch I found the feet of the first hanged man dangling not three feet from my face. I shrieked and nearly fell off my perch.

My heart hammered in my throat, but I did not have time to regain my composure. I could hear men beginning to come up the hill. Someone shouted below—I had been spotted!

The next thing to nearly startle me off the tree was the first lightning crack of Bonehill's Whitworth. A horse screamed and died below me while I pulled myself to standing on my precarious branch and began to saw through the rope.

The rope was old, rotted, and dried out. It gave easily and the body quickly vanished from sight.

I tried to ignore the squelch it made upon impact.

Gunfire still rattled below, and I took heart as I climbed up that Maddy and Graham were still alive and fighting.

An errant wind turned the next body to face me and to my dismay I found his eyes and lips had been sewn shut. The face strained at the seams, desperate to release the gas within. Dry heaving, I held fast to the trunk with one hand and cut him down.

"Some of 'em aren't getting back up, Charlie!" Toby shouted. "Keep going!"

Hand over hand, and foot over foot, I climbed further. The next body would place me a good twenty feet above the ground, and I still had to make my way around the tree.

I worked the circumference of the trunk, walking across the base of branches. As I reached for the branch that would bring me to the next body a hole exploded beside me.

I screamed, felt my grip vanish, and my body slip. The world jumped up several feet and a branch kicked me in the gut knocking the wind from my lungs. But I held on, damnit. I held on.

Agonizing for breath, I struggled to pull myself upright.

Again I climbed. I'd dropped three feet. There weren't branches to take me directly up to where I'd fallen, so I had to pass under the body, come up on the other side of it.

The lips and eyes of this fellow were likewise sewn shut, but that hadn't stopped something from digging at him. The meat of the jaw had been picked clean off and now the bone itself dangled only by the remaining sewn flesh around the chin and lips. I was quick to end his indignity.

Morbid curiosity held me rapt as I watched him bounce off the branches below and finally burst open against the ground. The sighed caused my vision to swim and I almost let go of the trunk.

Something inhuman roared below me, and a heartbeat later I heard the clear tone of Maddy's scream. From my vantage point I could see most of the town. I stared down in time to see fully half of a building collapse—the one Maddy'd taken to hiding in.

My heart stopped until I made out the shape of her, the skirts of her creamy orange dress gathered in one hand, rushing up the hill toward us. Three men chased after— Graham, and two of Raleigh's boys.

"Cut the bodies!" Graham shouted. "Cut the bodies, boy!"

Startled back into myself I cast my gaze around for the next closest hanged man. This one swung his jig on a branch two feet above my head and six feet out. The others had rotted and bloated, but this one's skin shriveled around the sewn eyes and mouth, pulling the stitches tight. I fought down my gut's roll.

Ignoring the gunfire crackling below me I began my ascent again. After a short climb I straddled the branch with my legs and began to scoot forward. The knife rattled in my teeth and fogged with my breath. My nose itched and drool slithered out the corner of my open lips.

Think of Samuel. Think of the posse. Think of the others below me. Everyone is counting on me.

I reached where the rope curled over the branch and started sawing away. A moment later the body crashed through the branches and collapsed in a heap in the dirt below.

"That's four," I said to myself.

I began to climb again. I was now as high as the tree could support, and the next two bodies were slung on branches at this level around the tree. The air around me hummed with something just beyond hearing, something more sensed than felt. It prickled at my memory.

Unasked, my thoughts wandered to a muggy summer night in Minnesota. I had clawed through the cobwebs in a crawlspace and watched just ahead of me as Ginny Catskill worked her skill. As Ginny Catskill mouthed the spell that would mark Samuel with her death. Magic—that feeling would be magic, thrumming in the air like a plucked string.

"Five," I panted.

Again the inhuman roar. I looked down and saw one of the two remaining bandits rolled on the ground, clutching his gut and screaming holy terror. The second approached Maddy where she stood firing her rifle. He twitched with each bullet plugged in his body.

It was him, the man with the monstrous, deformed arm, making that terrible noise. Now that I knew what I was looking at, I wondered what creature could have donated that hideous black arm, so like a man's but so different.

At his side a cavalry saber rattled. He dropped his spent gun and gripped the saber, drawing it.

Useless from my height, I shouted. "Maddy, no!"

The man rushed her, raising the saber high. His arm bulged and twitched as though something crawled in the muscle below. For a moment it swelled thick with ropes of unnatural muscle and it came down.

She threw up her rifle instinctively. Against any other man the rifle might have done it. The saber sliced through the barrel, clean.

A fraction of a second later Graham's hand grabbed her by the collar and pulled her clear of the blade's arc.

The air rang with the sound of the Henry's barrel bouncing on the gravel. Maddy stood, stunned, only for a moment. She raised the shortened rifle one more time and fired.

The bandit's head snapped backwards and he collapsed, gripping his eyes, screaming.

"The hanged man, you idiot!" Bonehill shouted. "Cut down the last body!"

I rushed as much as the swaying branches would let me, crawling around the tree to the last dancing figure. Again I sawed at the rope, and one last time the rope snapped. The air snapped with it and that terrible hum in the air silenced. For miles around us clouds of black birds rose from the woods and the grass.

Below the bandits screamed their last, expiring in the dirt they had unhallowed with their actions. The world fell calm once more.

I made my way slowly to the ground, picking branches with care, dropping only when I needed to. When I reached the ground I saw Graham, Bonehill, and Maddy sitting on three headstones, catching their breath. Maddy held something in her lap, and as I came close I saw it was the beautifully etched Henry.

The cut had been clean; leaving only a little jagged metal behind. She hefted it, admiring. A half smirk rose on her face. "I like it. Unorthodox. I could hide this under my skirt and no one'd ever know I was packing lightning."

"I suggest having a gunsmith see to it first, Ma'am,"

Graham said, cleaning out the cylinder of his pistol. "The barrel has likely suffered damage in the cut that could cause harm to your person."

I looked at the three adults, and then around the graveyard. "Where's Toby?"

The air split with the crack of a pistol and Toby's scream.

At the sound of her voice the three of us were up and running, guns drawn, before we even knew what we were doing. The sound came from the far side of the cemetery, opposite of the town. We saw the man the moment we came around the hanged man tree.

He was ragged, filthy—one of Raleigh's boys for sure. He was shirtless and slicked with sweat, as if he'd been working all morning, but his skin was the color of ash now. He looked like he'd been bleached out, except for the pinprick of blood welling at his heart.

Powder smoke rose from the rifle in Toby's hands, and fear froze her face. The two looked surprised—surprised to see each other, surprised to see she'd killed him. His hand rested on the butt of a pistol, half drawn from its confederate holster. Half drawn, with the thong still tying it down. He never could have withdrawn it without removing that thong.

The bandit fell to the ground, gasping like a fish. As we watched, his body broke out into a dozen bullet holes, knife cuts, and what looked like the mauling of a bear. Signs of the half-life he'd lived after Raleigh's gift appeared all over his quickly rotting flesh, and from it crawled flies.

"Stand back, Charlie," Bonehill said, planting a hand on my shoulder. "The other two did this as soon as they died."

The flies spewed from his wounds into the sky in a chorus of angry buzzing, and dispersed into the morning air. Unbidden, a shiver crawled up my spine.

"They were dead, but they weren't," I said.

Bonehill nodded.

"Looks like he was digging up a grave," Maddy said walking past him once the flies were gone.

Toby seemed to have found her voice again. It was shaky, and she fell into the grass, her wobbly knees failing her. "I found him hiding in it when the fight was over."

"What would Raleigh want with an open grave in the middle of nowhere?" Bonehill asked.

The wooden marker would only tell me what I needed to know in retrospect. It read: *In Loving Memory, Savannah Clayton*

"It's beautiful!" Maddy clapped a hand to her bosom, inhaling sharply.

When I crawled to the rim I saw what she meant. Chests and bags piled one atop the other at the bottom of the grave, and scattered all over them were gold coins, bars, trinkets of silver and gold, leather satchels of bank notes, and fine jewelry. It was Raleigh's horde.

"Two years of robbery sits in this grave," she said, voice full of wonder.

We stared down into that grave hidden in the yellow grass that came up to my knees—that grave planted in the little Kansas town that does not exist anymore. Two men, a woman, a girl, and me.

A mere glance at their faces told me each of us, man, woman, and child, was contemplating what could be done with the thousands of dollars buried in the grave. The thought was highly appealing—I could set myself up with a fine suit of clothes, dozens of suits of clothes! And a beautiful white horse, and a matched set of nickel-plated revolvers with pearl grips. And books…thousands of books! Oh, I missed books.

"Raleigh was expecting to add sixteen thousand more to his horde today," Graham said. "So he sent a man here to open up the grave."

No one disagreed. We each stared into that grave, deep in our own thoughts. The only thing to break us from our reverie was the sound that came with the breeze. The rolling pop of a dozen guns going off. One by one each of us looked up, shaken out of our fantasies, staring into the distance.

Chapter Twenty

The Lieutenant

Bonehill reached beneath his shirt and pulled out the iron Charlotte ring dangling from its leather thong. It hung in the air from his fist, but when I looked at it I saw it did not hang pointed at his feet, but leaning in the direction of the noise.

"What is *that*?" Naked, material lust shone in Maddy's eyes.

"Not yours." He said with a warning tone.

"They're close. That must be Hickok's men and the gang."

"Did Hickok chase Raleigh or did Raleigh chase Hickok?" Maddy asked.

I shook my head. "It doesn't matter. We have to go help them. Samuel needs me."

Perhaps a mile off we could see the silver feathers of smoke beginning to rise from a copse. Maddy chewed her lip, glancing between that copse and the money pit before us.

"Saddle up," Bonehill said, turning away from the grave. Toby and I turned with him, but Maddy hesitated.

"If he breaks away and comes to take the horde the process starts all over again."

"Maddy," I pleaded. "We need you and Mister Graham. You're good in a fight and I know the posse was probably outnumbered. Samuel needs you."

"Not that he would ever admit it," she muttered. She tore her gaze from the grave and nodded, brushing a flyaway curl from her face. "Alright. Let's go."

I ground my teeth all through that ride. There were spare horses left from the men who had pursued us—horses enough

171

to carry us each. I hadn't realized the extent of the group chasing us until I saw the bodies laid out, victims of Maddy's trap. Each sat as if nursing an ache.

Bonehill's ring drew us inexorably toward the copse. As we rode, the distant pops turned into the harsh cracks of true gunfire. Gradually the time between discharges grew longer and longer.

To my right Maddy rode a confident sidesaddle, her skirts swirling in the breeze. Graham rode beside her with a gentleman's posture, revolver ready in one hand. To my left Bonehill held my old Sharps like an Indian's war spear. With no Whitworth cartridges left, Bonehill had hastily abandoned it beneath the hangman tree before we left.

Toby rode in the saddle behind him. The rifle rattled in her hands, and her face was grim white, but her hair streamed behind her as a flaming standard of war.

The copse loomed before us as we drew near, wreathed in fine smoke. The only noise I could hear above the rolling thunder of our hooves was the crack of guns. The woods obscured the gold of a muzzle flash and my horse screamed.

"They see us!" Bonehill shouted.

Everything happened at once. My stomach lurched as my horse dragged me toward the ground. Bonehill, Toby, and Graham raised their weapons as one and fired into the foliage. A delicate gloved hand swooped down and snatched me from the falling saddle.

"Help me help you," Maddy growled as she strained to pull me up with her. I clawed at the saddle and managed only to flop across it on my belly, the horn digging into my side.

She pressed close and I felt the horse turn. Around me the three remaining horses turned in unison to ride the perimeter of the copse. More fire came, peppering the air, but it was met in kind. Inside I heard the struggle renew itself. Fresh clouds of smoke filtered through the leaves.

As we circled the copse, a familiar figure stood out from the underbrush and waved to us. It was one of Hickok's deputies, guiding us in. Bonehill stopped us short of the copse, ordering everyone off the horses. We crossed the rest of the distance at a crouching run.

Underbrush thinned almost as soon as we crashed through it. A smoky fog covered the patch of woods, cut through the center by a running creek. On either side men hid in ditches and against fallen trees. So many bodies were pressed flat to the ground that it was impossible to tell the living from the dead and dying.

"Where the hell have *you* four been?" Hickok shouted above the din.

We fell in nearby, dropping to the dirt and crawling across to fallen underbrush.

"Weakening Raleigh's position," Bonehill said.

"The hell does that mean?"

"Anything weird happen?" I asked.

One man, the bully from this morning I realized, looked up with a wild fear in his eyes. "They just a'started exploding with flies and flashes of light. All the rumors was true! They's demons!"

"Not anymore," Maddy said. She hefted her shortened Henry over the edge of her log and popped off a shot. Someone screamed.

"What are the numbers?" Bonehill asked, beginning to slip a paper cartridge into the Sharps.

"Dead," Hickok said, his voice shaking. "So many dead. They routed us at the station. We had to flee, but they kept chasing us."

I met Tom Bonehill's eyes, and I knew he and I shared the same thought. *They didn't get the coin yet.*

A voice began to shout above the staccato of discharging weapons. Slowly the pace of fire slowed to a stop and I could make out the voice. Raleigh.

"Saaaaamuel! Samuel Clayton, you God-damn traitor!" I was sure his voice was shaking. "You know what I want. Just walk on over here and these men live."

"He's still alive," I breathed. Beside me I spied Maddy release a sigh of relief.

A shape shifted in the grass, and I realized it was Samuel.

"The hell does he want?" Hickok asked. "Didn't he get enough with the gold? What's your stake in this?"

No one answered the sheriff's questions. Every eye was on the space between Samuel and Raleigh. The bandit leader was sitting up now, blood streaming down his filthy face. The cocky grin was gone, but a zealot's fire still burned in his hateful gaze.

"Good of you to join us," Samuel called. He rolled onto his back and I saw him looking in our direction. His face was smeared with dirt, mud and blood mixed in his beard.

"Sorry to keep you waiting," Bonehill shouted from his cover.

"You did good. Hey, Tom?" I saw him fish brass cartridges from his pocket and begin to slot them into his rifle.

"What is it, Sam?"

"You and Garner take good care of Charlie."

The words stole the wind from my lungs. I couldn't even shout my protest as he rose as a ghost into the smoke-choked air. Daniel would tell me later he saw a sight that moment that he'd never thought he would see again:

Lt. Samuel Henry Clayton, marching toward the enemy.

He strode forward, rifle raised, firing into the enemy ranks and men fell. In the chaos that ensued Raleigh screamed the order to fire, spittle flailing from his lips. The survivors of our

174

posse must have seen something in Samuel's march as they rose and began to fire back. Lead peppered the air and still Samuel marched.

Fire, reload.

Fire, reload.

He shot with one step and chambered with the next.

With no hope I pulled the hammer back on my Dance and joined the fray. Men fell. Screams cut through the sound of the battle. Clouds of angry black flies rose to the canopy above.

Raleigh rose from his cover, laughing. "Alright, if that's how you want it, traitor!"

Samuel shouted above his own rifle. The sound was strangled, a sob of fury. "*We were all traitors, Barker!*"

Bandits and posse alike, we all fell silent to watch.

The bandit king's reply came wordless. He threw his pistol to the dirt and charged across the stream. I expected Samuel to do the same.

Raleigh leapt at him, grabbing for his neck. Samuel shifted and spun, and the stock of the Henry came up. The thick sound of the blow across Raleigh's skull echoed through the copse.

He dropped from the air, landing on his face in the dirt. Without another thought Samuel dropped the rifle and pulled his Remington.

His voice trembled, and I knew if I could see his face I would see tears. "Goodbye, Barker."

"Goodbye, Sammy, old boy."

Samuel fired.

The woods were quiet for a long time after the echoes died.

Chapter Twenty-One

The Secret Ring

Hickok didn't believe a damn word of what we said. I wouldn't have either—every bit, every syllable of it was false.

When he finally released us—Samuel, Daniel, Bonehill, Toby, and myself—from the cramped cells in Abilene we found the two dapper gentlemen waiting for us outside his office. They followed us out into the street where Samuel stopped and turned on them.

"What?"

One man, with a cleft chin, approached curling his exquisite mustache. "You've done your country a great service, Mister Clayton."

He extended a hand, which Samuel did not take. When it was clear no return gesture was forthcoming the man withdrew and tucked it in his pocket.

"Didn't do it for my country," Samuel said.

"Of course not. And not for the money either, clearly. I believe any bounty claims were forfeited on Barker Raleigh, am I correct?"

Samuel ground his teeth, but his tone was civil. "Regrettably."

Daniel broke in, his gentle voice always the medicine for bad tension. "Gentlemen, it's a pleasure to see you again, but the only reason Sheriff Hickok concluded his business with us is because a dear friend of ours is leaving town today and we wanted to see her off."

As if on cue the whistle of a train unfurled over Abilene.

"Ah, I see," said the man with the mustache.

His companion, a more amiable looking fellow with a

black bowler cap nodded toward the station. "Once you've said your goodbyes, we'd like to see you. We're staying at the Palace Hotel."

They shook hands with Daniel and Bonehill, though Samuel still declined. On the way to the train station Bonehill spat in the dirt and looked around at the rest of us.

"What d'you suppose they want?"

"They looked like law men," Toby said.

"Nothing good," Samuel said. "We got our things. Let's just say goodbye and leave town."

"I still say we should collect the gold on the way out," Bonehill said for the twentieth time, adding, "Just think of the look on Jefferson's face when we bring it back to Charlotte."

Once again the thought of a nice set of clothes and a brand new brace of nickel-plated pistols danced in my head. And so many books...I could have a collection to rival Daniel's!"

"Ain't ours," Samuel said, spitting. "We let Hickok know where it is on the way out."

"We could take just a little," I said.

The sour look he gave me silenced me immediately. Seeing my expression, he softened a little. "Charlie, I'm sorry. We need money, true. But it ain't our money to take. It belongs to the folk who've been robbed."

I nodded slowly, not looking up at him. Some small part of me felt ashamed for my greed. "I know. It just would be nice."

The train whistled again. We rounded a corner, and there was the narrow, thin ticket office and the platform. A small crowd of people waited to board, and from that crowd I picked out her parasol easily.

"There!" I said, pointing.

I suppose she heard my voice, as she turned at that moment, her face lighting up.

"Gentlemen! Oh, I'm so happy to see you." At visible

protest from Graham, Maddy dropped off the side of the platform into the dirt and rushed toward us, carrying her skirts in her free hand. The old butler came up behind, hauling three carpetbags in hand.

"Charlie! Tom, Daniel, wonderful to see you. October, you look lovely. Comb that hair every day and you'll melt hearts when you're older."

Toby's cheeks burned red, and I thought she glanced in my direction. For my part, I didn't meet her eyes.

Maddy stopped before Samuel. They stood less than an arm's length apart, so close and intimate yet separated by an ocean.

"Samuel," she said.

"Miss Irving."

"I'm glad to see you came out well."

He cleared his throat, looking at the ground.

"If you'd allowed yourself to die," she continued, "I'd have conducted séances day and night. You would never have a moment's peace in the next life."

"...Barely give me a moment's peace now, woman."

Faster than he could react, she leaned in and gave him a peck on the cheek. While he still stammered, she smiled and turned toward the platform.

"I was right—you were a boon to him."

I blinked. "What? How?"

"You kept him level, you kept him on our side."

Before I could say anything else she continued. "Continue to take good care of him, Charlie. I want him whole the next time we meet." She twirled her parasol, waving a delicate gloved hand over her shoulder.

I whipped off my hat and waved it to her, and Bonehill, Daniel, and Toby did likewise. Samuel stared at her departing back, saying nothing, looking thoughtful.

"Hell of a woman," Bonehill said.

"Pain in my ass," Samuel said, though there was no malice in his words.

Jericho howled with a lonely wind. Gusts threw small eddies and curls of dust into the air from recently collapsed buildings and structures long since burnt to the ground. Three men, a girl, and a boy stood over an empty grave and stared at the bare dirt beneath.

"Was it Raleigh?" Daniel asked. "That seems impossible. Perhaps some of his men escaped."

"They rounded up everyone they found," Bonehill said. "They're set for a court date as soon as the judge arrives in town."

"Love to be there for that hanging," Toby muttered.

I wasn't watching them. I watched Samuel who paced the grave. I could see the clockwork turning in his mind, see the thoughts already beginning to form. He scanned the ground, then the area around the grave.

"Oh, Goddamnit."

A shovel stuck upright from a mound of grave dirt, and from the shovel a scrap of creamy orange cloth fluttered in the wind. An envelope waited where the shovel bit into the dirt. I followed his long strides as he marched over to it and tore it open.

"Boys, I'm terribly sorry. The money is long gone now, but I promise to put it to good use. Samuel, I hope this won't douse your flame for me. I shall always and ever be incredibly fond of you—even when you drive me mad. Love always, Madeline Irving. Postscript: Enclosed find the calling coin."

Daniel jerked, startled. "What? I had secured it!"

Samuel glanced at him and continued reading. "I had a moment of conscience." He upended the envelope and sure enough Wither's coin fell out and into his palm.

Bonehill threw his hat to the dirt. "Son of a…"

"We don't say a word of this to Hickok," Daniel said.

Crumpling the note up, Samuel said, "Agreed."

A long way off I heard the sound of a train's whistle as it crossed into Missouri.

In the cattle town of Hays we found a jeweler and a locksmith willing to take unusual requests. We stayed just outside of town for the few days it took to for the commission to be complete. But on the third day when he stepped out of the jeweler's building holding the bundle, Daniel gave a pleased smile to the other two Knights.

"Will it work?" Samuel asked.

Daniel's jaw was thrust out with a pleased grin as he held it up for our inspection. The commission was a leaden lock box bound at the four corners with thick iron.

"If this does not contain the coin, nothing will," Daniel said.

Bonehill spat a wad of black chaw in the dirt, his face soured. "We should chuck the damned thing in the river and be done with it."

Knowing what things lurk in rivers, the idea made me uncomfortable.

Samuel was likewise against the idea. "Tom, we bargained our souls. We're better off keeping one eye on the good Duke, there."

The three of them fell silent. Nearby, a train whistle pierced the sky.

Checking his watch, Daniel said, "Well, gentlemen, we have a few hours before the train east leaves. How about we have a drink to salute a job well done?"

"A drink to say goodbye?" Bonehill said.

"A drink to commemorate a lost companion," Samuel said.

Daniel opened the lid on the lockbox and Samuel pulled a small pouch containing Wither's coin, dropping it inside. Snapping the lid shut, Daniel pulled the key from his waistcoat's pocket—a silver key, plain, with seven tines. Business concluded, we each picked up our saddlebags and walked down the street to a saloon.

The atmosphere of the saloon was quiet, the only light coming in from the curtained windows. A few souls hunched at the bar over mid-day drinks while the bartender dusted the liquor shelf.

"We don't serve pups," the bartender said when he spied Toby and I.

Samuel said, "They'll take theirs watered down."

"I said we don't serve children."

Before Samuel could threaten the man, Daniel broke in. "We're toasting a deceased compatriot. Have a heart, friend."

The man grumbled, but he acceded.

We settled ourselves at a table, and no sooner had drinks arrived and the Brothers toasted than a pair of shadows fell over our communion.

"Gentlemen, don't think we'd let you get away that easily."

The two dapper gentlemen stood over us, faces spread in wide, oily smiles.

"What do you want?" Samuel's face darkened at the sight of them.

The man in the bowler hat gestured to a pair of empty chairs. "May we?"

Samuel grunted, but the men took it for a yes and helped themselves.

The man with the very fine mustache slipped a folding cup from his jacket and helped himself to the bottle at the table. The man with the bowler hat fitted a pair of spectacles over his eyes and regarded everyone at the table.

"Gentlemen, over the last six years my associates and I have been taking note of some, well, extraordinary murders."

That earned the Charlotte Knights' attention.

"Who are your associates?" Daniel asked.

"We'll get to that in a moment." The man with the bowler hat sniffed, a nervous habit. "Looking into these extraordinary killings, we thought we might have a case of men addicted to killing. But the closer we looked the more bizarre the circumstances were found. In fact, we became alerted to a problem most men would only scoff at."

He began patting his jacket looking for something. The man with the fine mustache whipped a piece of paper from his own jacket and passed it to the man with the bowler hat.

"Ah, thank you Mister Lodge."

"My pleasure, Mister Hayward."

"Let's see…" Hayward unfolded the paper and began to read off of it. "June 1865, a horned creature, half man and half wolf, decimated a Confederate cavalry unit in the town of Charlotte, North Carolina. July 1867, travelers visiting Whimbley, Mississippi found the entire town slaughtered. They also said that all the victims had sharpened fangs where their teeth had once been. December 1867, a 'Carnivorous goat man'" he chuckled, "attacked a settlement of Dutch immigrants in Pennsylvania. Sixteen dead before the creature was reported killed by a portly man with a coach gun."

Mister Lodge peered at all of us over the rim of his cup, smiling.

Hayward continued. "September 1868, a negro wedding party in New Orleans is disturbed when the mute adopted sister of the groom viciously attacks the wedding party. They're stopped by a white man with a scar along his jaw. They later told authorities the adopted sister was a fish woman from Lake Ponchitrain. Winter 1868, an Ohio town reports unusual deaths and disasters in relation to a gigantic man with moth wings. Shortly after, a group of men show up and are purported to have stopped this winged man. February 1869, a Union Pacific worker reported being rescued from 'a gigantic monster with eyes like fire and the antlers of a deer' out in Wyoming.

"1870, a cargo shipment of Egyptian artifacts bound for Chicago goes missing, several die surrounding the disappearance. Days later in Springfield a man shows up and kills another man wandering around wrapped in bandages. Here: last summer was a busy one. Some kind of tiger wandering around killing lumberjacks in Minnesota—a man strings up and brutally kills a few whores and the killings stop. A Catholic congregation in Missouri is invaded by a 'demonic apparition' and an army of ghosts, stopped by a small boy. And here, Alton Illinois, a man-eating bird the size of a horse is terrorizing the countryside until a man and a boy bring it down with a cannon."

Hayward folded the paper and tucked it into his jacket. "These are just a few of the reports we've investigated. We've followed your career for a long time. But tell us about yourselves."

We were dumbstruck. Samuel was the first one to speak, staring at the glass in his hand. Beneath the table I knew his hand was resting on the grip of his Remington. "Sounds like you already know about us. Tell us a bit about you."

Lodge leaned in, his face splitting in a wide grin. "We're the men who want to pay you for what you been doing already."

"The offer is simple," Mister Hayward said. "We can provide you with what information we know when something occurs. When you have dealt with the problem the U.S.

183

Government will be happy to pay you a bounty for your trouble—starting with and including the death of one Barker Raleigh."

No one but Bonehill spoke, and all he could muster was, "Damn."

After a moment of silence Daniel spoke up, his voice weak. "Who are you? You don't look like Army. Are you Pinkertons?"

"We're several steps above Pinkertons, Mister Garner. We represent a ring of gentlemen handling the country's most sensitive problems—problems we want kept quiet."

Daniel's eyes went wide. "I thought the Culper Ring was a myth."

"I would think a man whose slain harpies would be a little more believing of myths, Mister Garner."

Daniel choked on his drink.

Mister Lodge hefted a carpetbag from the floor beside him and began rifling through it. He pulled out three envelopes. "These are offers of contracts—things that need dealing with. We have more for your friends, but no means of contacting them. And this," he pulled a wad of bank notes out and set it on the table, "is for services already rendered."

Bonehill's hand clamped down on the roll of money and he began counting it even as Daniel passed an envelope to him. Samuel's envelope sat on the table before him untouched, so I took it and opened it.

"God damn!" Bonehill said. "So does this mean we're a part of this Culper whats-it?"

Lodge laughed and Hayward simply shook his head. "Hardly. But if you're willing, we can form a mutually beneficial partnership. We're even willing to discuss bounties on creatures you find through your own volition. President Grant believes a monster-free America is more conducive to the achievement of our national destiny.

"So, whom shall I contact about long term partnership?"

"What's it say?" Samuel whispered to me.

My eyes flew over the writing, scanning it for any information. "They want us to investigate rumors of an entire mining town literally vanishing from sight. A place called Silverton."

"Literally vanished?" Samuel said aloud.

Hayward nodded. "Just after mining companies began to take an interest in the town. No one comes back from Silverton. No one can even *find* Silverton. Ahh, Mister Clayton that is interest I see on your face plain as my hand before me. I assume we have an agreement, then? Whom can we contact about a partnership?"

Carnacki the Ghost-Finder

The Drowning Puddle

J Patrick Allen

I had received an invitation from Carnacki to join him at his home for a luncheon. Rarely seeing my friend so often during the day I accepted and arrived at the prescribed time. We shared a quiet meal of soup and cheeses, he and I, before repairing to the study.

"What is the special occasion?" I asked as he poured me a coffee from a silver pot.

"I arrived home from a red light séance this morning," he said. "Late. I thought I should very much like to collect my thoughts and enjoy an early meal."

With that small preamble he invited me to sit and launched into his tale.

"You've doubtless heard the name Peter Borrowych of the Clerkenwell Borrowyches. Yes, I can see it in your eyes. What you may not have heard is that Borrwych has been having a devil of a time keeping servants in his employ. I had not heard this myself until I arrived at his house at nine o'clock last night for a small party and séance.

"The house in question is along a particularly flush stretch of Farringdon. He threw a rousing party, and the company was delightful. The small hiccup in the evening began when we were finishing our meals. Normally, this would have been the cue for Borrowych's man Winceslas to step in and begin the process of clearing away the course for the next meal, but he did not arrive. Indeed, Winceslas had vanished entirely when Miss Starling had sent for a particular wine from Borrowych's cellar.

"Borrowych became very understandably cross, but I must tip my hat for the man did not shout nor scream. Indeed, he held onto his patience rather longer than I might have. At the time when the dinner guests were beginning to grumble our gracious host picked up a small bell with which to call his man and gave it a slight ring.

"All eyes watched the door expectantly, but when no sight of Winceslas became evident Borrowych deigned to call out.

"'Winceslas!' he called. And still there was no response. Finally Borrowych excused himself from the table. This was when Captain Pevensy leaned over to inform me of the run on servants Borrowych had been experiencing.

"'Three in the last two weeks alone. Jove, but you would never think the conditions here so bad.' It was in such a state that our man Borrowych was brought low to go hunting for his manservant during a party. I pitied the man, but we thought very little else of it until we heard the scream.

"I stood immediately and ran to help and quite naturally the chatty dinner party followed, doubtless looking for new gossip. The hideous sound of the scream came from an open door leading down into the black of the house's cellar. I ventured down the stairs, seeing the wan light of a hand torch. From below you could still hear the sound of Borrwych crying out. 'Winceslas! Winceslas, no!'

"There in the cellar we found him. Borrowych had sunk to his knees at the far end of the chamber and seemed to be sobbing to the floor. When I went over to the man I saw he had collapsed by a shallow puddle of water, no deeper than a hair's breadth.

"'Jove, what is it?' I asked him.

"Borrowych pointed to the puddle. 'Something has dragged Winceslas to his death. I saw him thrashing in the water, gasping for air!'

187

"Despite the premise of our presence in the house tonight, some heard his claim and there were dubious looks passed among the lot of them. One callous fellow went so far as to laugh, if only to himself.

"Now in the absence of such noise some unconscious part of my mind started to feel something queer about the room. As you know I always keep an open mind, and it was this that allowed me to detect something unsettling. It was enough to raise the hair on the back of my neck.

"'Borrowych, come come. Yes, that's a good man. Tell me, how many servants have you lost?'

"'Since I've moved to this house? Eight, sir. They always leave without telling me why.'

"Eight indeed, I thought to myself. Borrowing his hand torch I began to make a full inspection of the place. With the help of the others we managed to turn the cellar upside down in no time. It was then that I began to find certain articles: A cuff-link here, or a bracelet there. Jewelry or personal effects, nothing quite expensive but all of it likely dear to the one to whom it belonged.

"Many of these effects could be found along the wall where I would find leaks of water seeping through the bricks. There were not always puddles of water, but I stepped in enough to feel suspect. Each leak, each puddle was only found along the southern edge of the cellar.

"At last, unable to find more and all of us feeling quite tired, we began to leave. Our most gracious host saw each man and woman up the stairs with a quiet gravity and dignity. I was nearly at the door myself when I heard another shout of surprise from Borrowych. Looking down the stairs I could see a great wisp of lambent mist.

"I rushed down the stairs to join him, only to see an apparition most gruesome in appearance reach out from the mist. She—for it could only have been a woman—grabbed Borrowych by the wrist and dragged him deeper into the cellar, toward the southern wall. The creature was all skeletal, dangling with rotted flesh and rotted white dress and veil flapping in the still air.

"I grabbed him by his free hand and pulled against her, but her bony claws sunk deep into his arm and dragged with inhuman strength. I called for help from those above and heard the rush of footsteps as the rest of the dinner party joined the fray. There were gasps of terror and trills of fright from some of the women present but two men, Captain Winslope and Mister Hawthorne, formed a chain behind me and started pulling.

"We ceded inch after inch to the rotting horror however, and soon she began to drag Borrowych beneath the depths of the pool at the far end of the room as though it were an ordinary pond.

"I ordered the others to brace their feet and I did so as well. We hauled, hard, watching Borrowych's face vanish beneath the surface of the water. And then there was hope. Two more men from the party joined the line and pulled. Inch by straining inch we retrieved our host from the water's ab-natural depths. The ghost released her prey at last and the six of us flew back in a mighty pile, Borrowych landing atop as king of the hill, soaking wet and stinking like a sewer.

"The creature gave a distant wail of despair as she sank below the surface of the puddle, and soon all was quiet but for the sound of our huffing and of Borrowych's terrified gibbering.

"The chiming of the hour saw the entire dinner party upstairs surrounding our host. He sat in his chair, a blanket wrapped around him, while I thrust a cup of tea (and a splash of whisky) into his hands.

189

"I silenced the room and their questions, and we watched while Borrowych drank the tea. At last the hot drink and fine liquor worked their magic upon his system and he ceased his shaking. He looked me in the eyes, seeming to have aged ten years, and asked me, 'What the devil was that thing?'

"'That is what I would very much like to know,' I told him. And then I asked, 'Your servants, have they all left at night?'

"'Without warning, yes. At night all of them.'

"I stroked my chin, casting an eye to the kitchen where the door to the dread cellar stood. 'I think we may safely assume that this creature has absconded with the majority of your servants, though some may merely have been chased away. And no word of this has ever reached your ears?'

"Borrowych shook his head, staring into his empty cup. 'Some of the servants expressed discomfort in the house to Winceslas shortly after being hired, but he would scold them for fools and days later they would simply vanish. It was perplexing.'

"'How long has this been going on?' I asked him.

"'Oh, perhaps six months? I began to lose my old house staff, and then went to the hassle of hiring new staff. Jove! Poor Winceslas. He served my family since I was a boy.'

"After questioning Borrowych I set a plan to order. I had one of the guests bring me a good length of rope from the house's tools, and I hailed a cab to retrieve my own usual instruments from home, so necessary to the preservation of life and spirit. Upon my return we secured one end of the rope about my waist and the other end to the banister at the top of the stairs. Thus protected I set about creating chalk circle around the puddle and making within it the signs of the Saaamaaa Ritual. I lit my candles and smudged thoroughly with garlic, but at the end of it I did not utilize my electric

190

pentacle. I realized to do so would be more hazardous to the living than the dead, owing to the sopping nature of the space being warded against.

"I stayed for a few hours in the dark of the cellar and watched. About One O'Clock the mist began to rise again, and I heard that distant mournful call. She rose again from the water and attempted to glide toward me. It was only my own efforts at abjuration that saved my life, I tell you now. She was confined at once to the space within the pentacles. It was only when she was thus contained that I got a good look at her.

"The apparition was reduced to rotted bones and mangled flesh. The dress and veil would once have been white but now bore deep brown and yellow stains, and by Jove she stunk. The smell crossed the barriers and filled the room with the impression of fish and sewage. But I recognized her for what she might have once been. She was a rotting bride.

"Satisfied that she was thus contained I took some pictures for my own edification and put the camera away, retreating upstairs to catch at least a few hours of sleep. In the morning I gave orders to Borrowych to bring in an army of men with shovels and pick axes.

"'Why on earth would you need that?' he asked me.

"'Our spirit's manifestation indicates she is much older than the house you occupy, and I suspect that we will find something beneath the floor of the cellar that will reveal all.'

"When I arrived in the cellar to check on the pentacles I found that the circle was quite empty. Supposing the creature temporarily retreated to the dimension from whence she came I began to inspect the wall by the circles. I only noticed the way the creep of water had broken my chalk lines a mere moment before the fog arose again.

"With a cry of fury the spectral bride grasped for me from

191

within a mote of mist. It was only my natural quickness which kept me from the same fate suffered by Winceslas and the rest of Borrowych's household staff. I retreated up the stairs to await the fullness of daylight and the arrival of the hired men.

"So it was, early this morning, that men hauled brick and dirt away from the wall and the floor. It was only two or three feet down that we discovered a passageway running beneath the house. And from that passageway came the stink of sewage and the sound of fast flowing water.

"Of course! Yes, it was the River Fleet buried beneath Farringdon some years ago for our own protection. When the sun still shone upon it, it was not unheard of for murderers to hide their deeds by casting the bodies into the river. And so I suspected it was the case here, a murder committed long ago by men who might not even survive today. I climbed down into the river passage with a hand torch and cast the light about, searching for something which might cause manifestation of one of the Aeiirii.

"I waded ankle deep into the fetid waters and at last found what I was looking for. Six months ago it must have snagged against a jagged brick and come to a rest. It was the mere bones of a hand, the flesh and clothing long since rotted away. But something remained glinting in the dark beneath our very feet—a golden ring. I took the ring and presented it to Borrowych, ordering him to have the bones burnt to ash and the ring melted down immediately. Secure in the knowledge that he would have the problem eliminated I came home to catch a last few hours of sleep and perhaps a bite with a good friend."

Carnacki smiled at me upon that and I lifted my glass to him in salute.

"And you're sure that will eliminate the problem," I asked him.

He fixed me with a dubious glare. "This is not mere superstition Dodgson. This is science. As long as he followed my orders he will never be troubled by the creature again. Alas, if only he'd thought to call me beforehand we might have saved many more lives."

At the end of our conversation Carnacki saw me to the door. We shook hands and exchanged our farewells with promise to meet again soon. As I left his residence I thought to myself, "What an incredibly sad story, to be killed on your wedding day and be left for all eternity seeking the ones who deprived you of such joy."

Acknowledgements

Thank you, Jennifer, who egged me on.

Thank you, Samantha, who was my sounding board.

Thank you, Mom and Dad, who fed me as many books as I could read.

Thank you, Nikki and James, who rolled the dice on me.

A Note on Tarot in 1872

Popularized as a method of divination by French Occultist Jean-Baptiste Alliette more than a century prior, Tarot crossed into the English-speaking world late in the 19th century. In 1861, one Kenneth Mackenzie visited France and partook in the teachings of occultist Eliphas Levi. Returning home inspired, he began to work out the plans for a new occult lodge. The work he laid down would be used after his death as the basis for the foundation of the Order of the Golden Dawn.

Tarot did not become truly wide-spread and popular in England until the mid to late 1880s, though it is not unfathomable that those with certain connections (and a good deal of free time to explore said connections) might have come in contact with the principles prior. Indeed, spiritualism and the occult were blossoming in Victorian society during the period of this book.

The form of Madeline Irving's tarot practice is fictitious, cobbled together from fractured bits of historical information and consultation with practitioners of cartomancy. It is designed to bear primitive semblance to Tarot as you might experience it today. Whether you can use it to tell fortunes, I cannot say.

Personally, I doubt it.

J Patrick Allen grew up exploring the American West with his family. He climbed mountains, fished, camped, visited the family cattle ranch, and explored a castle. Author of the *Dead West* series, JP writes about the monsters we take with us. Every week you can listen to JP on the *Rocket Punch Radio* podcast on iTunes, Stitcher, and TuneIn, where he and his friends hold round table discussions about all things geeky. In 2016 his story Dragonfly Shadow was awarded Best Short Story from the Pulp Ark New Pulp Awards. When he's not hard at work, he and his wife can be found curled up with a beer and a book or game.

Preview

Midnight

By M.H. Norris

Dr. Rosella Tassoni is not a ghost hunter. She is not a traditional forensic anthropologist either. Her goal is to solve the crime hiding behind various myths, legends, ghost stories, and internet games gone wrong,

Taking a chance and deciding to go into business for herself, Rosella finds herself on a case that could make or break her career before it has a chance to start. Will she find herself in over her head?

All The Petty Myths is an anthology that features the first mystery featuring Forensic Mythologist Dr. Rosella Tassoni. This collection also features stories from Marc Sorondo, James Bojaciuk, and D.J. Tyre.

DR. ROSELLA TASSONI looked over the auditorium full of half-asleep freshman and quickly remembered why she *usually* only agreed to lecture upper-level courses.

"Since the beginning of time, man has told stories. When a written language came along, these were written down. Some would surpass their own cultures, becoming what we know to be legends. Today we call the study of those legends mythology. Every culture has their own distinct legends, yet many share a similar foundation. Max Müller considered these legends 'a disease of language,' but clearly they're something more. I prefer Tolkien's explanation for legends in his essay 'On Fairy-Stories,' originally delivered to students very similar to you. 'The history of fairy-stories is probably more complex than the physical history of the human race, and as complex as the history of human language.'"

Rosella clicked the slide over before reading the quote. "What are the origins of, as Tolkien would call them, 'fairy-stories'? 'I am too unlearned to deal with this question in any other way than with a few remarks…It is plain enough that fairy-stories (in wider or in narrower sense) are very ancient indeed. Related things appear in very early records; and they are found universally, wherever there is language. We are therefore obviously confronted with a variant of the problem that the archaeologist encounters, or the comparative philologist: with the debate between independent evolution (or rather invention) of the similar; inheritance from a common ancestry; and diffusion at various times from one or more centres."

Turning away from the screen she studied the crowd. "Tolkien is considered one of the greatest fantasy writers in the history of mankind. His books are still widely read and have even inspired a popular MMORPG."

That comment helped her pick out the gamers in the audience by their grins. She could tell a couple of them were thinking about playing that as soon as class was over. In fact, the way one boy's head shot up, she couldn't help but wonder if she looked at his screen if she would find Middle-Earth.

"But, more than that, he was one of the great philologists, with an intense knowledge of language's history—and the mythology that has always clung to it. *Gilgamesh*, after all, is our earliest surviving written record. Tolkien acknowledged Müller's quote though and had this to say, 'Max Müller's view of mythology as a 'disease of language' can be abandoned without regret. Mythology is not a disease at all, though it may, like all human things, become diseased. You might as well say that thinking is a disease of the mind. It would be more near the truth to say that languages, especially modern European languages, are a disease of mythology.'"

That caused her to chuckle. "I prefer to agree with Tolkien on this. After all, that quote is how I earn my living, in a sense."

As she walked across the stage, clicking through slides, she eyed one of the students. He slipped into the back of the lecture hall, border-lining the time that it was socially acceptable to arrive late. Which was, also, the time it was polite for Rosella to be late. She'd earned her doctorate. At least according to the old myth—Rosella preferred to be on time to speaking events, not in the mood to waste not only her time but the time of those listening. The student quickly opened his laptop and tried to look attentive, but his shoulders were tense yet his face portrayed a different story. His face appeared to be relaxed but his clenched jaw told her he was stressed and a little over focused on the task at hand. Not only that but she could see his wire from here. He must be new, he was too tense. That or he hadn't been warned that she was pretty good at reading body language. But seriously, Quantico was slipping if they thought that act was covert. She assumed he was wired simply to test him in the field, in a safe situation. Baby's first op.

"Some stories are to teach a lesson, it's the reason we have fables and how Aesop became a household name. Others are fun stories to tell around a campfire or a childhood sleepover or to be turned into the next Disney movie."

"Others take a darker side, or rather people choose to let them." Another click another slide.

"Serial killers, immortalized in this day and age by the influx of crime dramas which seem to occupy most major networks. People are obsessed with the idea of the forensic sciences."

Now she had their attention.

"Sometimes, the two meet. Killers think they can hide behind the myths. Forensic Mythology if you will."

A student in the fourth row raised her hand and Rosella nodded to her. Being called on by a guest would at least give her a good story. She was one of the ones who'd perked up at the mention of *Lord of the Rings Online*. Her Mac was plastered with stickers—a TARDIS design that went out with the sixties, a *Metropolitan* press badge reading Smith, and Mara Jade holding a pink lightsaber aloft; it was clear this girl knew her science fiction and fantasy. Her straight posture and over-eager expression let Rosella know that this was probably one of her friend's better students.

"So, you're saying that most urban myths aren't true?"

Rosella smiled. "That's not my job to figure out; that was more something Margaret McConnell studied to learn, and I direct you to her books. I prefer to leave that to other people to argue over. I have to sort the very real killer from the myth."

Another hand, this time from a boy who had looked bored until she had said "serial killers." Then his attitude changed rather quickly and the combination of that, along with the book by Temperance Brennan in his bag, made her wonder if he knew how much was real and how much was fiction. Though at least he was reading one of the more accurate adaptations. Nodding to him, she was partially curious what question he'd come up with.

"How do the two manage to come together? Mythology's just stories. Forensic Science is an actual science."

It was a question she often got. With a nod she clicked a slide. "Most people wonder how I manage to see the two combined. Who here has gotten one of those annoying chain emails, the ones that say if you don't pass it on you'll bad luck or meet an untimely demise?"

Hands all over the auditorium went up. They usually did when she asked the question.

"A few years ago in Dallas, Texas one of those went around. The thing was, people who didn't pass it along met said untimely demise."

She clicked a slide and showed a set of three victims. Each one had received a single bullet wound. A tarot baring the reverse chariot was laid beside them. "All of our victims had received that email within twenty-four hours of their death and for a while that was our only tie-in. Forensic science—the wound delivered at point blank, the presence of the card. Fornensic mythology—the email, and the card itself. When reversed, the chariot tarot card means bad luck."

"Did you catch the guy?" Someone near the back asked without raising their hand.

"Eventually. He managed to kill five victims before we were able to nail down his location. But when killers use something like these superstitious emails or urban legends, they often use them as a mask to hide their crimes. Some people are so focused on the legend coming true that they refuse to see what's right in front of them—a human being."

"So the myths aren't true?" The over-eager girl repeated her earlier question.

"Once again, I didn't say that. It's not my business to prove or disprove them. Though I will say those annoying emails are probably the creation of someone who had too much time on their hands and more than enough access to the internet."

That earned her a few chuckles. "Forensic Mythology is an emerging sub-classification of the forensic sciences. And while many of my colleagues don't think it's practical, I do know that it has helped to save lives and bring peace to victims."

Another hand went up and she nodded to the person about halfway back. "But why mythology? What made you think to combine it with the forensic sciences?"

201

Rosella launched into her traditional lecture, smiling at how once again, she had managed to get the students to steer the conversation to where she wanted to go. Of course, they didn't realize that that's what just happened.

The rest of the class passed quickly and soon enough students were packing up to rush off to their next class, a hot date, a procrastinated study session, or one of the seemingly endless things students could do. Finally, the tardy student from earlier made his way up, carrying a copy of her latest book in his hand.

"You know, you can drop the cover now. A tip, when your body language sends mixed signals, a trained eye is going to notice."

The kid's face dropped and he shrugged. "They said you were good. Does that mean you won't sign my book? I actually really enjoyed it."

Rosella let out a chuckle. "I'll sign it. I'm assuming somewhere in that bag there's a file for me?"

"A case came up and my superior wanted you to take a look. He thinks it might be up your alley."

"Your superior knows that, officially, I'm not here." Rosella let out a sigh, the extremely long to-do list she had made for this trip to DC suddenly seeming unattainable.

"According to him, it's right up your alley Also, he said something about covering your hotel here and rescheduling any appointments you miss to take a look."

She turned to Professor Alicia Walter, an old friend of hers. "I might have to take a raincheck on that coffee."

A LARGE CAN OF SALT—the brand gave away that it had been bought at the local dollar store—sat beside a pillar candle in a glass drawer. It was probably of the same origin of its twin, which tipped over beside a taped silhouette. It gave Rosella a hint of the sad story that had played out here, a couple of days ago.

Rosella rubbed over a bloodstain with a gloved hand and didn't try to hold in a sigh.

"I don't get it." She turned to see the Sheriff Kristopher Peake studying her studying the scene. "I've seen it so many times and I still don't get it."

She pulled the case file out of her bag and looked at the picture of fifteen-year-old Ashley Coats. Honor Roll, freshman at Huntington Prep, involved with the SGA. A fairly large amount of friends on Facebook, a couple hundred followers on Twitter. Nothing indicated that something like this could happen to her.

But that silhouette proved otherwise.

Five kids, five crime scenes, all within just a few hours of each other on a Friday night. The salt and the candle gave away that it was a ritual of some kind. What had Ashley gotten into?

She grabbed the file again as she heard someone enter the room.

"Who is she?" a voice asked the Sheriff.

"Someone the FBI called in. Apparently, she's an expert on cases like this."

"And we weren't consulted?"

"We have jurisdiction here."

Rosella looked at the photos of the crime scene and noticed that Ashley was cut open, hence the large blood stain on the floor. "And we have a group of dead kids and no evidence that this *isn't* going to happen again so if you are going to act like small children can you at least do it outside and let me work? Thank you."

She wandered into the kitchen, mentally ticking off different cultures, different rituals, but it was always a mix of what was and what wasn't there. She opened the cabinets until she found the spices. Garlic, oregano, cilantro—nothing outside the usual household collection. Shutting the cabinets, she walked around the kitchen peeking in the pantry.

"All the internal organs were missing when the coroner came, right?" She walked past the group of law enforcement officers to the other side of the house. "From all of the victims?"

"Wasn't a pretty sight."

Rosella nodded as she continued to wander the house. Matches littered the floor in a couple of places. Looking at the notes, she searched for the time of death. The coroner estimated it to be around three in the morning. She added discussing a few things with him to her mental to-do list.

That time of death did narrow down the ritual some more.

She wandered into the bathroom, peeking in the drawers and cabinets. But nothing in Ashley's bathroom showed anything outside of the ordinary for a girl her age.

The parents' room was first, but looked basically untouched. "Where are her parents?"

"Staying with some friends until after the funeral on Wednesday," an officer who had been bagging something in Ashley's room answered.

"Have they been here since?"

"Briefly."

Rosella peeked inside the mother's closet, the faint hint of designer perfume lingering on her clothes. The closet was all women's clothes; the husband's must have been in a guest room. There was another match off to the side of the master bathroom floor.

She made her way into the girl's room, not surprised at the hottie-of-the-month's face all over her walls. CDs took a shelf where books should be, and her laptop sat on her bed. With a groan, she saw all ten seasons of *Supernatural*. Of course she watched that show. Victims in Rosella's line always seemed to. Next to it sat a couple of seasons of *American Duos* and Rosella quickly shoved away the nagging feeling that she'd forgotten to TiVo it.

Right now, she needed to focus.

As she crossed the threshold, she looked down and saw a piece of paper. In flowing script was Ashley's name and a drop of blood.

That *really* narrowed it down.

Rosella knocked on the door three times. Wood.

There were a couple more matches by the door.

"Make sure you bag up the matches we're finding all over the floor."

Coming into the room, she looked under the bed, between the mattress and the pad, between books, and in the drawers. Besides the things at the door, this room could have belonged to any teenager.

"What's the verdict?"

Rosella turned to see the Sheriff leaning up against the doorframe of the parent's room.

"Sometimes, when figuring out what ritual, it's a mix of what's there or what's not there."

"A ritual?" The Sheriff looked troubled. "What do you mean?"

"The salt, the candles, it was a ritual. There were several options that would require both of those. Actually, most preternatural related, modern rituals require both."

"Preternatural, don't you mean supernatural?"

Rosella crossed her arms as she felt her eyebrow reach for her hairline. "Would people stop misusing that term? This was a *preternatural* ritual."

Seeing the blank look on his face—she sighed, and slipped into lecture mode. "Preternatural is used to refer to actions that are demonic in nature. Supernatural refers to acts of God. The word is often bastardized into meaning 'things beyond nature.'"

"You're saying she was practicing witchcraft?"

"I am not."

"Summing this up, demons had something to do with this? But she didn't practice witchcraft."

Staring the man down, she decided to cut him a break, for now. "Ashley here unknowingly engaged into a preternatural ritual. In fact, I'm fairly certain I know which one it is."

"What is it?"

Rosella made her way back into the family room where the silhouette still sat on the floor. "It looks like she summoned the Midnight Man. And he won the game."

Preview

The Mouth of the Ness

By William Meikle

The first novella in Josh Reynolds and James Bojaciuk's series *Cryptid Clash!*, William Meikle's The Mouth of the Ness shows us what emerges from the Wyrd when Vikings go a-raiding.

TOR TORSSON STOOD at the dragon's head as the longboat made its way by oar up a foggy firth. They were reaching shallower shoals but his concern was not with possible obstacles in the water, but with his friend, Skald Orjan who sat on the deck rolling the bones and muttering to himself. The seer had been lost in the Wyrd all morning, and the rest of the Viking crew were starting to mutter, seeing the crippled mystic's behavior as an ill omen for the raid to come.

"What do you see, Orjan?" he asked. To Tor the youth at his feet would always be Orjan Persson, the boy who'd almost died in a rock fall and his lifelong friend, not the crippled youth who fought like a Berserker and spoke to the Fates that the other men saw. But neither facet of the Skald was talking—he just kept muttering, almost under his breath. One of the words was 'doom', but Tor wasn't about to relay that to the rest of the Vikings—not on his first sail as Captain.

Besides, it was the Skald's vision in the Wyrd that had brought them this far. The Scottish highland capital, Inverness, was somewhere in the fog ahead. Skald had seen it in a vision, even while sitting by the fjord at home—the town and, beyond that at the head of a long inland fjord, an abbey that hoarded great wealth of gold, silver. There was more—a secret that Orjan could not see, but knew was worth a King's ransom could it be taken; a worthy prize for a Viking raid.

It hadn't taken Tor long after Skald told him of the abbey to persuade his uncle to let him undertake the journey—both Tor and the Skald had more than earned the right on their last trip out. There, in the wild arctic lands to the east of Sweden, the Skald had discovered the true depths of his tie to the Wyrd, and Tor had saved a whole crew with his strength, courage and wits.

Now here they were, approaching Scotland after two weeks at sea, Captain and Seer, brothers in blood and glory, with a prize in their sights. The trip itself had been uneventful, but the closer they got to the Scottish shores, the more Skald retreated into himself, called into the misty dreams of the Wyrd and travels in the mystic—places where Tor could not accompany him. This time he had been gone for several hours, and Tor was starting to consider a forcible awakening when Skald finally looked up from the bones and nodded.

Tor hefted his sword—a last gift from Ragnar before their departure, and tapped twice on the dragon's head. It was done softly, and would be heard no more than ten yards away in the fog, but the sound echoed enough in the long timbers that the crew took heed and stopped rowing. The longboat drifted inside a flat calm in thick fog, trusting to the Skald's sight that they were close enough to Inverness to need caution from here on. Tor had never been given cause to doubt his friend's counsel—and had it confirmed yet again when they heard the sound of a church bell toll in the fog—a matter of several hundred yards away at most.

They had come across the expanse of the Northern Sea, and were now as close they could get to the highland capital without being noticed. Now they must do little but wait for nightfall, and their chance to creep through the strait at Inverness and into the loch of the Ness, where the

208

prize awaited them.

They broke bread and had some ale, still drifting in the fog. The crew was in fine spirits despite having rowed for several hours against the current. As ever, they were respectful of Skald when he was close to their captain, but Tor saw many give his friend the sign of the evil eye as he passed toward the rear of the boat where he liked to eat—alone. Tor sighed inwardly—if he could give his friend peace, he would, at any price that might be demanded—but there was little sign of peace or rest in either of their immediate futures, and he forced his thoughts back to the task at hand as the fog darkened around them. Somewhere beyond the mist, night was falling—and the Viking was about to begin properly. Despite his worry for the Skald, Tor felt his excitement rise and his grip tightened on his newly gifted sword.

There was fortune and glory ahead of them—and he meant to take as much of both as was to be had.

THE SKALD CAME FORWARD again as a breeze came up and the fog cleared to show the last of the sun going down beyond a town ahead of them, where the north and south shores converged.

"The strait is narrow—but there will be no moon," he said. "Our passage should be simple enough if we are quiet."

"You have seen this?" Tor asked, and for the first time in days the Skald laughed.

"Yes—I looked up," he said, then winced and clutched his leg. The damp always pained the old wound, and at times Tor wished it had been he, not Orjan that had been pinned under that rock, if only to spare the hurt he knew his friend suffered. But the Skald waved Tor away when he expressed concern.

"It is no worse—and no better—than it has ever been. And it will be that way until I go to the Wyrd for the last time, so there is no use in me complaining. Come—let us see if we can get beyond the town—I will get an hour and more of rest once we are on the loch itself."

The two of them stood at the prow as the twenty-four oarsmen—all well practiced in silent rowing, took them slowly toward the town, whose firelights were now showing red against the darkening night.

They kept to the south side of the channel—the shoreline there was densely wooded and looked to be uninhabited, and they crept as close to the tree line as was safe in the dark so that their silhouette would not be seen against the sky. Tor held his breath as they past within arrow distance of the keep on the hill that stood guard over Inverness township, but there were no warning cries; no fires were lit. Within minutes they had left the town behind. Ten minutes after that the strait widened to more of an open river—it was tidal at this point and, as they had come in on the rising current of the night tide, they negotiated the shallows with ease. Five minutes after that the longboat emerged into the wide breadth of the loch itself and they were able to unfurl the sail as an easterly breeze got up at their back. The sailcloth snapped in the wind and the longboat bucked, once, then started to make good time under sail along the length of the loch.

"How far?" Tor asked.

"It is on the north bank—a couple of hours sail in calm waters, which is good news for our chances of success, as the later we arrive, the less prepared they will be for an attack."

"It does not matter how prepared they are," Tor said with a grim smile. "You say they are monks? I have never heard of any man of the cloth prepared to stand against a Viking raid—I doubt these Scots are any different to their counterparts in the South."

But Tor was not about to abandon all subtlety or caution. He placed a man on watch on either side of the prow—there were only scattered settlements along the loch side, rarely more than two or three fires in each one and a mile or more between each one. But he preferred to err on the side of caution—at least until the prize was in sight.

Skald went back to sitting on the deck just behind the dragon's head, his bad leg outstretched, straight in front of him like a bit of dead wood. He called Tor down to join him, putting his head close so that no one would overhear.

"We have talked of the prize, you and I—but we have not talked of the hidden secret—and now I believe we must, for I have seen further into the Wyrd on my most recent sojourn there—we are sailing into trouble."

It was Tor's turn to laugh.

"We are Viking. We are always sailing into trouble."

Skald did not smile in return.

"There is indeed a prize ahead—but there is also darkness there—a writhing, smothering, monstrous darkness. It hangs over the abbey like a great serpent, barring all my attempts to see past it."

Tor did not much like the direction the conversation was taking.

"Was it not you that showed us this prize in the first place? You said it was a great thing—a wonder that would make our names as Vikings. Do not say we should turn away now."

Skald spoke even more quietly, scarcely more than a whisper.

"I merely propose caution…"

Tor laughed again, and repeated his earlier words.

"What need have we for a surfeit of caution—we are Viking. We will take that abbey, have their secret, and be on the way home with the outgoing tide in the morning. Take heart, Orjan; great deeds await us. They will sing about us in song in ages yet to come."

Tor saw Skald decide to keep quiet—he knew that look of old—a desire not to annoy a friend. But if there really was dark danger ahead, Tor had to know, for the sake of his crew.

"Tell me," he said. "Tell me what you are not saying. And if it makes you feel better about it—your captain commands you to speak."

That did get him a smile.

"Since when has that ever worked with me? But you are right—as Captain here, you need to know—but I fear you might not understand, for it is a thing of the Wyrd."

"You mean it is something of the Gods—something from Asgard itself?"

"It is certainly of the mist—and more of Niflheim than Asgard. Whatever it is, it is strong, it is fearsome—and it protects the secret of the Abbey. Perhaps we might be content with the gold and silver? For this other thing—it is beyond my ken—beyond anything I want to ken."

Tor saw the worry in his friend's face, and clapped Skald on the shoulder.

"I will take whatever counsel you offer, my friend. If the abbey coffers have sufficient gold and silver, then we will have that, and that alone. It will surely be enough—I too have no wish to meddle further in the ways of the Wyrd— certainly not this far from hearth and home."

Skald fell quiet again, and Tor left him to his thoughts. He stood at the dragon's head watching the shores as the longboat glided, almost silently, up the long, wide, loch under a dark, cloud-covered sky. Once again he felt excitement rise at the prospect ahead. It was well known among the Norsemen that most of the White Christ's abbeys held wealth. It seemed to Tor that the Mediterranean god was more interested in raising taxes and accruing wealth than any religion had a right to be, but if it meant more plunder for him and his people, he was not going to pass it by. Especially as this particular abbey, thought too remote and too far from the sea to be in danger, was so little defended—and so easily accessible with only a modicum of stealth.

He stood there for several hours, the only sound the snap of wind in the said and the soft lapping of wavelets on the prow. He drifted into a watchful state he'd learned on long nights on guard on his home shores—somewhere between dozing and wakefulness where his eyes saw but his mind wandered, only coming alert at anything untoward in his field of vision.

Finally, some two hours after making sail, Tor gripped his sword hilt tighter as a darker shadow showed against the night sky on the north shore ahead of them. They had reached their destination.

He tapped lightly on the decks with the sword—twice—and the crew got the message. They dropped the sail. The steersman at the rudder—with the aid of the slight breeze—brought the longboat in a silent drift ever closer to the shore.

The abbey was built atop a rocky outcrop that jutted into the lock from the north shore. There were no defenses visible, and no windows showed any light—it was merely a dark block of stone with a tall tower at one end, although the walls were high and thick, and there a single iron gate on the south side to mark the only entrance.

"Caution, Tor," Skald said—but the young captain's blood was up at the thought of glory. The anchor was dropped, and Tor leapt out of the boat even before it hit bottom, splashing through thigh deep water toward the dark shore. The rest of the crew followed—even Skald, who Tor had wanted to stay in the longboat, but who insisted on joining the attack.

He waited on the shingle shore until the crew was all disembarked. He did not need to discuss tactics—each man knew his job and knew the goal. He showed them his sword, pointed it at the abbey, and as a man they moved quickly off the small beach onto the approach to the building itself.

There was no defense mounted—the gate was not even locked—it creaked open at a single push and within seconds the party of Vikings were inside the abbey itself. At first Tor thought that their arrival had been anticipated and that the abbey had been emptied, far all seemed dark, quiet and silent. Then he spotted the flicker of candlelight against two tall windows. On investigation they found two dozen monks in the chapel—all praying, none of them armed or inclined to put up any fight. Tor left four men watching them, then scoured the rest of the building.

Skald had been right. They found a small fortune of gold and silver plate in an anteroom of the chapel, an underground storeroom filled with barrels of mead and ale, and even a heavy wooden chest full of a variety of different coinages, much of it in Spanish gold.

There had still been no attempt to stop them as the Vikings lugged their spoils up into the main part of the building. Tor was about to declare the raid a success and head back to the longboat with the plunder when Skald put a hand on his arm.

"There is the other matter—it is in the tall tower overlooking the loch. I can feel it draw at me. Whatever it is, it is strong in the Wyrd—stronger than anything I have ever felt."

"Do you still counsel that we leave it alone?"

Skald shook his head.

"I know not—but now that I am here, I fear having whatever it is at out backs on the return sail. It might be best to have done with it now, while we can. But it should just be we two—the other men would not understand. And it might be perilous."

Tor nodded. He ordered the crew to get their spoils back to the longboat, and with Skald at his side and his sword in his hand, they headed for the tower.

Preview

Bel Nemeton

By Jon Black

Spinning out of its success in Nicole Petit's *After Avalon*, Jon Black's *Bel Nemeton* expands on the world and characters from his novella.

In this, the first novel in a five-book series, artifacts are unearthed that seemingly imply Merlin was a real man. But what should be an ordinary, if controversial, press announcement is attacked by gunmen willing to do whatever it takes to steal the artifact, leading Vivian Cuinnsey on an international chase to uncover the magician's greatest secret—Merlin's tomb.

Prologue

THE DREAM WAS OVER. Tears streaked down his wizened face as he surveyed the landscape. Bodies lie strewn throughout the Camlann Valley. Chill winds carried the stench of smoke and blood into his acute nostrils. He arrived too late, taking too long to escape the bewitching Nimue's imprisonment. His escape was a tale worthy of Arthur and his best knights, but it didn't matter. He had failed in his duty as his king's advisor, wizard, and friend.

In his mind, Myrddin saw how the battle unfolded, as surely as if he had been there. Without the benefit of his counsel and his knowledge of tactics learned from the old Romans, Arthur and his men had simply charged, trusting that valor and strength of arms alone could carry the day against the traitorous Mordred and his Saxon allies.

He envisioned Camelot's finest as they charged the Saxon's fluttering banners along the broad, flat valley. Recent rains swelled the ancient River Cam, threatening to

215

flood its banks. As the king and his company advanced, their formations grew ragtag and discipline frayed. Caring only about being first into the fray, the men ignored the high ground on either side of them. And so they remained ignorant of the surprise Morgana and Mordred concealed there. Myrddin would have done the same had he been in Mordred's place. He shuddered at the thought.

Still, Arthur and his knights had turned the tables, won the battle, and destroyed themselves in the process. Britain's king lingered for several hours afterward, so Myrddin was told. But the old man had not reached the Camlann in time to say goodbye.

He could not believe Arthur was gone. Arthur, whom, as a swaddled infant, Myrddin had cradled in his arms and sang to. Before Uther. Before even Ygrayne. Gone. Now, Brittan was without her king, the foe vanquished, and Mordred no more. Myrddin did not know if Morgana numbered among the living or the dead. He hoped it didn't matter. Without Mordred, Morgana amounted to nothing. Didn't she? But there would be another wave of Saxons. As far as Myrddin could tell, there would *always* be another wave of Saxons.

"Myrddin."

He looked up, it was Cei. The solemn and sober knight numbered among the handful of Arthur's host not only to survive the battle but remain, mostly, unscathed.

"Is it done?" Myrddin asked, wiping the tears from his face. Cei nodded gravely. Myrddin noticed the wound to the knight's face. His cheek would always have a scar. It would match the one on his heart.

How strange that, at the end, it should come down to the two of them. There had been no love to lose between Myrddin and Cei. Neither made any secret of it. Myrddin found the old warrior tiresome, self-righteous, moralistic, and utterly mirthless. He could only imagine what Cei must think of him. Despite that, each man understood and trusted the other's unconditional love for Arthur. That had been enough to unite them.

Cei surveyed his surroundings, searching. "Bedwyr?"

Myrddin shook his head. "Not yet returned," he clarified, lest Cei should misunderstand him and fear another of their company had fallen. Cei had completed his task, as Myrddin knew he would. He hoped Bedwyr possessed the mettle for what he'd been assigned. The venerable cavalier reminded Myrddin more of a grandfatherly otter than a fearsome Knight of the Round Table. With his gentle voice and kind heart, Bedwyr deserved birth into a better time and place. And yet, they also gifted the knight a curious kind of power. Even dead-hearted Mordred had possessed a soft spot for Bedwyr.

Time moved in circles, Myrddin reflected. It had been the three of them, Cei, Bedwyr, and Myrddin, with Arthur at the beginning. And it was the three of them here, at the end. He had known it would be so. More years ago than Myrddin carried to count or admit, he had dreamed. The kind of dream that Bleys, his ancient mentor, taught him to always pay attention to. In his dream, Camelot burned. Stone. Mortar. The rock foundation itself. Everything consumed in flames. Camelot burned and it fell to the three of them to dispose of the ashes.

And so they had. His dream had come to pass.

Myrddin studied the knight, "What will you do now?"

Cei considered the question. "Stay here. Rally the others. Try to pick up the pieces. You?"

Myrddin, too, thought before answering. He plumbed the depths of logic and reason as well as his intuition for omens and portents. Though tempted by Cei's answer, he could not allow himself to go there. "Darkness descends upon this land," Myrddin pronounced, "and no man shall stop it. I shall walk the wide world searching for Arthur's spirit. And, if I do not find it, I shall simply go home."

"God be with you in your quest," Cei said.

"And the gods be with you in yours."

One

"**DAMN IT,**" Vivian Cuinnsey swore at her computer. Once again the document she was preparing failed to format properly.

"Everything okay, Doc?" Grant, her graduate assistant, poked his head through the door.

"I'll get this. Eventually. It'll be fine."

That stretched the truth. Since becoming department chair last year, she had been immersed in a world of budgets, policies, and academic politics that bordered on vendettas. Keeping a department full of idiosyncratic Celtic Language scholars running was a full time job.

Then there was the graduate seminar she taught. Only one class, but an important one, complete with rubrics, lesson plans, and grading. Vivian thought the move from undergraduate to graduate studies was a bigger transition that going from high school to undergraduate. Both high school and undergraduate revolved around what you knew. Graduate school involved coming to terms with what you didn't know. A little acclimation went a long way in helping new graduate students adjust to that shift.

And, of course, Vivian functioned as her department's chief fundraiser and its public face, to the university's administration, alumni, and the world at large.

Now, she faced additional pressure from an impending meeting with an Irish-American CEO who, having embraced his roots, was considering a sizable endowment to her department. The document which had frustrated Vivian all afternoon was part of her campaign to make the donation a reality.

Another half-hour resolved the formatting issue. Sending Grant home for the evening, Vivian also prepared to leave. Checking email once more before closing her laptop, she was surprised to find a message from Dr.

Weldon Grassley, a venerable professor emeritus with her university's department of archeology. Well past retirement age, Grassley remained on the university's payroll and perpetually in the field at excavations throughout Central Asia.

"Dear Vivian, I found this at an excavation in Uzbekistan. I would be very interested in your thoughts."

The attached photo showed a stele, an upright stone plinth, bearing inscriptions in three alphabets. She did not recognize the top two. The first was all thick shapes and dramatic lines. Thin loops and lines characterized the second. At the bottom, however, she found the familiar Latin script Vivian encountered a thousand times a day, the letters used by English and dozens of other languages.

Though uncertain why Grassley sent the photo to her, it piqued Vivian's interest. Greek inscriptions, courtesy of Alexander the Great, were sometimes found that far east. Latin was another matter entirely. A glance told her that, while the script was Latin, the language it recorded certainly wasn't. That came as no surprise. Many peoples had borrowed the script of the far-reaching Romans for recording languages not previously written. Excluding the cumbersome Ogham script, that included her beloved Celts.

Unraveling the Latin script's phonetics, Vivian saw familiar patterns. They were far better suited to the tongues of long ago Britain, Ireland, and Gaul than to the dusty caravan routes of Central Asia. The inscription seemed to be some form of Insular Celtic, the language family to which all living Celtic languages belonged. The words preserved on the stone stele manifested distinctly Insular Celtic traits like verb-subject-object word order and inflected prepositions. At the same time, they lacked traits associated with the other branch of Celtic, the now extinct Continental Celtic family, such as a third gender form.

Having determined the inscription to be Insular Celtic, Vivian's next task was deciding to which of that family's two sub-branches it belonged. The Brittonic language family, still called "Brythonic" by some older linguists, included modern Breton, Cornish, and Welsh as well as their parent languages and a half-dozen extinct linguistic dead-ends. The Goidelic family of languages included modern Irish, Scottish, and Manx, all of which evolved from Middle Irish.

Dr. Grassley's inscription gave every indication of being Brittonic, specifically the tongue called "Common Brittonic." Between the Fifth and Seventh centuries, that language held sway from Scotland's River Clyde to France's Brittany Peninsula. After the Romans left Britain, distinct dialects of Common Brittonic began to emerge. Those dialects would one day become the separate languages of Breton, Cornish, and Welsh. Perhaps Cumbrian and Pictish, too. Opinions differed as to whether Cumbrian represented a distinct language or just a dialect of Welsh. And, while everybody had a theory, no one really knew what Pictish was.

Having, at least in broad strokes, placed the inscription's language in time and space, Vivian grabbed pen and notepad. Scanning the weathered letters again, she made a quick translation. Words she thought likely to be proper nouns were put into brackets while she offset confusing or unclear sections with parentheses.

The Great King [Tarkun] (causes to be raised?) this monument. (Unclear) house of the Great Counselor [Mirdin] in his honor. (Unclear) Great Counselor to King [Tarkun] for this (two-ten years?), formerly counselor to Great King [Arturus] of the sunset lands. With Great King [Tarkun's] blessings, [Mirdin] departs to the sunset lands to look upon (its?) green trees and endless water (one last time?).

The inscription was a potential bombshell. A career could be made, or broken, by those few lines in stone. But it might have implications far beyond that. A quick mental calculation told Vivian it was too early to call Uzbekistan. By the time she got home, made dinner, and settled in, it would be the perfect time to catch Dr. Grassley at camp before he left for the dig site.

LEFTOVERS PUT AWAY AND COFFEE IN HAND, she sat at her computer. Dart, Vivian's black cat, orbited her legs, occasionally staring up at her with his yellow eyes and big ears. She thought about the scrawny kitten he'd been when he first appeared on her doorstep, one ear inexplicably smudged with motor oil.

Initiating a video chat, Vivian was rewarded with the image of Dr. Grassley's birdlike features, mop of white hair, and thick black-rimmed spectacles. "Dr. Cuinnsey, I thought I might be hearing from you."

"Dr. Grassley, what have you dug up?"

"It is a puzzle, isn't it, my dear? We're excavating near a small structure the locals venerate as the tomb of a Sufi saint. But we've dated it to the Sixth century, a couple centuries too old for a Sufi." Grassley paused and cleaned his glasses. "Were you able to translate the Roman script on the stele? Was it Celtic?"

"It was. Common Brittonic, to be exact. And I was, most of it, anyway. I'm emailing the translation now. How did you know it was Celtic?"

"An educated guess. After making a phonetic transcription, I consulted the standard references and did some online research. Celtic was one of the few language families I couldn't rule out. So, I thought I'd see if you could shed any light on this little mystery."

"What are the other languages on the stele?" Vivian asked. "I didn't recognize either script."

"They are both in the Sogdian language," Grassley answered. "The first is the classical Sogdian script. The other is the slightly easier Manichean script. With the caveat that we understand rather less about Sogdian than

221

Celtic, they both give translations broadly matching yours."

That pleased Vivian. Of course, it didn't really answer any questions about the stele or its inscriptions.

"Sogdian is distantly related to modern Farsi," he continued. "The spelling of this word 'Mirdin' on the stele is equivalent to 'Lord of God' or 'Noble of God.' I imagine this would translate conceptually as 'pious leader' or something like that, which sounds like a title. But notice that the word already accompanies the title 'Grand Vizier,' or what you translated as 'Great Counselor.' So, I am inclined to believe 'Mirdin' is a name, not a title."

Grassley flashed a mischievous smile. "Of course, 'Mirdin' would also be phonetically identical to the Celtic name of the individual commonly called Merlin, wouldn't it?"

"Careful, Grassley," Vivian shot back with hard-earned caution, "You're about to open one of the biggest cans of worms in Celtic studies. The historicity of Merlin, or Myrddin in Celtic, is very controversial. Even the affirmative camp posits Myrddin is an amalgam of multiple figures stretching across centuries. Arguing for the existence of a single individual analogous to the character from mythology is a good way to end a career."

"An intriguing point, given the reference to the 'Great King Arturus' and the 'sunset lands.'"

Thrilled by those same implications just hours ago, Vivian was suddenly in no mood to discuss them with the elderly archeologist. Again, she cautioned Dr. Grassley about the rabbit hole he was circling.

"You can grasp the momentousness of uncovering Latin inscriptions in Uzbekistan," he told her. "To say nothing of ones used to transliterate Celtic. We're holding a press conference about the discovery next week. I'd really like you to be here in Samarkand for it."

Vivian thought it over carefully. "I'm going to follow this development very closely. But, at this point, I can't

222

justify taking time off from my department based on one find, no matter how unusual."

"Regrettable. I always enjoy seeing you. But I understand. I will keep you informed of any developments."

"One more thing, Grassley."

"Yes?"

"Not a word about the whole Merlin thing. Not one word."

Two

HER MEETING WITH THE CEO went well. If Vivian guessed right, and she usually did, a few more glad-handing sessions would secure the endowment. For now, she shifted to focus to preparing for next week's meeting with the board of regents. Secretly, Vivian dreaded these meetings. She felt like she remained on probation with the silver-hairs who managed her university.

During her first year as chair, Vivian attempted to modify her department's degree plans to make it easier for students to take courses in subjects such as history, anthropology, and sociology, as long as the specific class related to Celtic history, culture, or society. The idea made sense to her. Language, after all, did not occur in a vacuum. And the students seemed to like it. But Vivian drastically underestimated academic territoriality. The chairs of other language departments, fearful they would be forced into making similar changes, banded together to oppose her. Perhaps, in a few years, she would try implementing a more discrete version of those changes. For now, she still licked her wounds.

She had tried to put Grassley's puzzle, with all its bizarre implications, out of her mind. Tried with only limited success. Vivian spent more hours than she cared to admit attempting to date the inscription using telltale elements of its grammar and vocabulary. The latter,

223

especially, suggested that the stele was engraved at a time when Common Brittonic had already fractured into dialects that were in the process of becoming languages. Curiously, the stele included words distinct to more than one of those dialects. That might deserve more attention later. Her working hypothesis was that the inscription's creator had been well traveled and possessed a very idiomatic communication style.

Taking all that into account, in her professional option, the inscription on the stele dated from the mid- to late Sixth Century. The right era, it had to be acknowledged, for a historical Myrddin. She suspected strongly it had been the native language of whomever composed it. The writing seemed to reflect the organic fluidity of a language acquired from birth rather than the structured precision of one studied formally later in life.

Sitting in her office, writing up follow-up emails to the CEO and his staff, Vivian received another email from Dr. Grassley. "Excavated the structure today. Features are consistent with a dwelling not a tomb. Think you might be interested in the more…unusual…aspects of the interior. Yours, G."

Many photos were attached.

The first one showed a weathered stone building adorned with flowers, colorful scraps of cloth, and bits of paper. This was the structure Grassley referenced during their conversation, Vivian concluded. Using Dr. Grassley and the other people in the photo to provide scale, the building must have been about ten feet wide, a little taller, and maybe twenty feet long.

The remaining photos showed its interior decoration. The spirals and elaborate scrollwork certainly looked Celtic, but that could be coincidence. She knew the Sarmatians and Circassians used similar motifs. It wouldn't be surprising if another steppe culture of the same era, like the Sogdians, did as well.

The frescos were an entirely different matter. The enclosed environment and arid climate combined to create a perfect preservation climate for the paintings, their pigments applied directly to plaster covering the interior walls. Vivid blues of the ocean and greens of endless forests, neither found within a thousand miles of Uzbekistan, testified to that. And were those red deer and otters? One painting could easily be the white cliffs of Dover. The one next to it, the pink cliffs of Brittany. Another fresco could only be Stonehenge. Its trilithons and bluestones, accurately but artistically rendered, rising above Salisbury plain.

It all spoke of a man suffering profound homesickness in a faraway land.

Grassley's photographs of the frescoes concluded with a stylized portrait of a king, painted in the traditional Celtic fashion. The young man, clutching a sword in his hands, was at once both handsome and saintly. Vivian sounded out the Ogham inscription on the weapon's blade, "Caledfwich." That name would become Caliburnus and, still later, Excalibur.

"Grant, send an email to the regents. We need to reschedule the meeting."

"Sure, Doc, why?"

"I'm going to Uzbekistan."

www.ingramcontent.com/pod-product-compliance
Lightning Source LLC
Chambersburg PA
CBHW070731280626
47159CB00023B/3085